I AIN'T A GIRL
by Joseph E. Hecker

Published by HeckHouse Press

You don't know about me without...

-Huck Finn

When love and hate are both absent, everything becomes clear and undisguised. Make the smallest distinction however and heaven and earth are set infinitely far apart.

-Seng Ts'an, The Third Chinese Patriarch of Zen

L et's open with facts. Since you're crack'n' this, it's facts that there's been leaks. And altho you've probably already 'eared of me 'fore you laid paws on this therapeutic, it's safe facts you ain't 'eared my side, 'cause no one's bothered to creed my side 'cept Therapeutic Kate, and facts is they weren't s'pose to be open-view'n' this, but like my father's Chrysler, everything leaks. Thus, I'm gonna spill this under the 'sumption that it'll be tabloid in seven and that lumps have already forked the first chunks they 'eared and made it facts, even tho I'm creed'n' that I'm literally the horse's mouth. Most is still gonna bump contra on social and there's not nothing I can do 'bout that. That's 'nother fact—there's not nothing I can do 'bout what lumps post, but I'm propose'n' that you should also 'sider that every tale is multi-sided and if you're crack'n' this leaked therapeutic, maybe you're open door 'nough to consider my contra. You could be strat'n' inroads to flip me and some of yous is trolls plug'n' for out-of-context to bump likes, but there's the previous fact so I'm just gonna drive what I can drive and spit only true facts.

▲ ▼ ▲

ATT: Therapeutic Kate: I just wrote that open'n' in case others is prying and if it's just you, then most of the previous ain't relevant, but we've been working on trust and I ain't got it 100% yet so that's that.

▲ ▼ ▲

Let's open with what every lump hits wrong from the get: the cabin that no one can locale really were. It ain't no hallucination nor delusion. You can't locale it 'cause it ain't a place no more. The fire smoked it and then nature reclaimed what were hers to start and so maybe a dig site for some archaeological Pitt undergrads, but do archaeological Pitt undergrads even exist? Don't get me pontificate'n' on present tense higher education. Slide a cash stack their way and after four years of natty lites and touchdowns, they'll slide back a framed document to nail-hang in a broken one-bedroom while you sweatshop the Gap till you're octogenarian. But now I'm left field. Pardon. I run off topic. I don't 'tend to, but, figure, you try crank'n' part of your life with girl tits and long hair, not to mention a shrunken area, when you're a stone dude and watch how 'tween the lines you steer. I'll try not but times are when I probably will stray. Apology, future tense.

▲ ▼ ▲

But, the cabin that ain't a place no more. First, I'll drop a pin. There's a real locale called Schenley. You can search it up on Wikipedia. It ain't hard, but no lumps bother. They 'stead spit I deluded it. Search it and you'll eye that Schenley is an unincorporated locale in Gilpin Township, Armstrong County, PA, in the US of A. How hard was that to detective? With a slow connection maybe five ticks. Then you'd crack PA 2062 is the main and only serious inroad, and I can fact that 'cause PA 2062's the very same road my scooter motored me on when I skedaddled to start with and what I should have motored back out on after it all flamed out with the lamb'n' of the pig and Tumult and Tessie and Jessup, but we'll get there future tense.

▲ ▼ ▲

Schenley is edged by the Allegheny River and the Kiskiminetas River, which also is facts, but the cabin is nearer the Allegheny and the Allegheny's bank is where the canoe were. I've never actually been to the Kiskiminetas River, but I'll creed it's a mighty fine river in and of itself, but it's not important to my true facts 'cause it's not, so let's progress. The locale, Schenley, is the site of a rusted industrial complex 'long the Allegheny that posts dilapidated buildings that once housed the Schenley Distillery and 'gain this ain't important to the facts neither and I never actually explored none of this broke-down depression, but I drinks whiskey altho that's a recent wipe and past tense at the cabin with girl tits and long hair, not to mention a shrunken area, I weren't tippin' no whiskey. I know socials peg me a popper and a libator, but that were not true facts past tense and is only sorta true facts present tense, but present tense ain't what lumps desire to spill. So Schenley actualled only one source hold'n' it a locale and that were the Kiski Junction Rail which past tense hauled freight but present tense is one of those family-fun trains.

I'm only spill'n' this 'bout Schenley 'cause I want you to creed that it's authentic and that as an authentic place, it's as solid as any other authentic place to motor a scooter thru so's to gain the rural surrounds and then steer left down the ruts and motor into trees and plop when you hit a clear'n' that's probably overgrown with shoulder-grass and weeds present tense. If you traced that, you'd plop where the cabin localed. So that's a setting with all but a GPS to aid those Pitt undergrads to geolocate and post some contra, and that's the ace I can throw. So let's past-tense to high school and the day this whole mess commenced.

▲ ▼ ▲

In the house, other than a Liverpool FC flag and a couple posters in my room, there were only one wall hanging that weren't religious, and since it were the only one, I didn't even recognize it as secular till my Sacred Heart junior year.

One day in art, bored like a friendless monkey, I cracked a famous American paintings book. Don't hit facts wrong, I ain't into no art. I were eye'n' for penis tags that Jimmy V laid with a black Sharpie, but instead of Jimmy V's penises, there it popped—Andrew Wyeth's *Christina's World*. Under the pic were a paragraph 'bout how Wyeth done this painting in the 1940's which passed back when my grandparents were like eight freak'n' years old so a long past tense ago. Anyway, in the painting there's this crippled girl who I spec is Christina look'n' like she could benefit with some aid as she sorta ground-sprawls in the middle of this tawny field. She 'pears to wanna land at a pathetic farmhouse, and there's also an equally pathetic barn and shed. The buildings all scan misery. Why she'd wanna gain to them ain't comprehensible. The words wrote that Wyeth were hyped to paint this when he eyed this Anna Christina Olson crawl'n' 'cross a field. It's facts that this Anna diseased something called Charcot-Marie-Tooth which I ain't never 'eared of but 'gain anyone with a hook can search it up and crack it's this disease that shrinks muscle and deads sensation 'cross body parts. The book writing don't bother to mention if this Wyeth thought to step out and aid Anna. I spec I would've, but I ain't no artist and maybe artists have artist sensibilities. 'gardless, it registers a jerk move to eye Anna crawl'n' and 'stead of aid'n', to pop hype for a painting and then that painting virals and you blow to fame if you 'ready ain't fame and then lumps commence to screen cheap reproductions and one of those cheap reproductions locales its way into a frame and is hanged in my house, but I'm divergent from the main point. So much had went down since the day I realized that that cheap reproduction weren't religious—but it were that book with Jimmy V's signature Sharpie penises scrawled on near every page, that started all this—that started the lines of my world to fuzz and intersect like misprescribed spectacles. Facts, focus is challenge'n' with all the social 'round and add to that what 'curred to me and focus 'comes nearly impossible.

▲ ▼ ▲

I don't know why it never 'curred to me that this framed print which had hanged 'bove the mantle my entire days weren't religious like everything else in that house. I 'ssumed that the girl were some suffer'n' martyr or a saint in the Lord's service. So when I learnt the facts, I knowed I was gonna confront my mother 'bout it, but I still had Geometry and then soccer 'fore I'd be able to land home and do some confront'n'. Geometry were all 'bout triangles, and I were like and still is like who the hell cares 'bout triangles, but that's just what high school is—sit'n' thru class after class after class sneak'n' social peeks and text'n' with your group while the teachers pontificate 'bout triangles. At least high school has sports. I'd 'eared rumor that European high schools don't have no sports and that sounds like it would really sleep—all triangles and no sports. Like succotash with just lima beans.

When school released, I laced on my boots and hit the pitch where I immediately hit chippy with Greecy our center mid and the coach had to separate us, but I'm aggressive and competitive and he was clunk'n' so he deserved it, but I'm only mention'n' 'bout that 'cause it's important for you to know that I'm like this 'cause I ain't some flower that the trolls like to paint me. That too is facts you should vault. 'fore the girl tits and hair and the shrunken area, I rocked stone stud, and I were hard for girls and that's fact. You can even question Jessica if she were open to spill 'bout it, but she don't talk 'bout it so you'll have to ride with my facts here. But facts is that Jessica knowed the stone stud by tactile sensation, and I ain't claim'n' we conjugated, 'cause we didn't, but I would've if she would've but she weren't like that. She did know however I was a player just wait'n' to be buzzed in the game. But now I sound all protest-too-much and 'sides the story will out that a flower wouldn't had been grope with Jessica, but we'll back burner that for present.

▲ ▼ ▲

After practice I wheeled home to confront my mother. She's one of those devout Roman Catholics but future tense maybe not as devout or else more devout than healthy but that's digress.

▲ ▼ ▲

My mother disliked the Liverpool FC flag posted on my wall and now I had contra to throw her way. Even with the future tense devout too much, I still like my mother. Pause here 'cause Therapeutic Kate is want'n' me to dig where the dirt is loose, so I'll spade that I probably still even love my mother. But I were in high school then and in high school, I were stretch and I knowed better, even better than her. So even with the knowledge that my mother had been thru a spin cycle with my dad kick'n' and all, I decided to contra her anyway.

"Your father always wanted a daughter."

That were all she spilled when I contraed her.

"Dad always wanted a daughter?"

My mother plucked a Granny Smith and a core'n' knife. She were concoct'n' apple crisp for the Sunday potluck.

"Your father always wanted a daughter."

"I heard you; I just don't comprehend."

My mother middle-split the apple and started core'n' out the seeds.

"Peel or not?"

"What?"

"The apples. I know we always eat apple crisp with the skin on, but not everyone cares for that. So do you think I should peel or not?"

"Don't nobody care. The only people at those Sunday potlucks are so octogenarian they probably don't got no idea that they are even eat'n'. Skin or no don't matter."

"Paul Joseph Rizzo, mind your manners."

"Ma, what about the print? Dad always wanted a girl? That don't even make sense."

My mother middle-sliced another Granny Smith. She were gonna leave the skin.

"Ask Father Antonio, he'll explain it. There are some things too delicate for a mother to discuss with her son."

"Jesus, Mother, sometimes I don't know why I even try."

"Paul Joseph, you will not use the Lord's name in vain in my kitchen. Now go get started on your homework. Dinner will be ready at six."

▲ ▼ ▲

It past many days 'fore I plopped with Father Antonio. He were the assistant rector and the student dean, and I thought he were equal to a cigar butt. Me and my group Sharpied mustaches and horns on every pic we could locale of him. But, I RQD facts 'bout what were so FBI classified 'bout that cheap print hang'n' in the living room that my mother wouldn't spill.

I waited for the lunch room to mostly empty 'cause I didn't want nobody perched to eye me chew'n' with Father Antonio. When the room were fairly empty 'cept for a few freshman mouth breathers on lunch detention, I questioned Father Antonio if I could hit him, and he made like for me to plop.

Like I mentioned, everyone most detested Father Antonio, but unfortunately I had known him all my sixteen and he were like that uncle who's always 'round but who you don't never really chew with and think is sorta perv. Altho he baptized me, heard my first confession, gave my first communion, and taught confirmation, we ain't never done nothing together like fish nor play catch nor nothing of value like that. God, that would odor sour if we had, and 'sides imagine the rep I'd carry if facts like those were 'stablished. No, he were just a crank priest, and like everyone at Sacred Heart, we didn't expect nothing from priests and even tho he were 'round lots past tense, I didn't exactly know what relationship I were supposed to have with him, so I specialed in cut answers and avoidance.

He buried my father and during the six months past, 'gain unfortunate for me, he often grubbed Sunday dinner with my mother and me and on the side I'll spill that at least my mother learnt me table manners and this lump must not of had no mother to learn him 'cause he grubbed like a cow and RQD a napkin hang'n' from his collar so as to not soil his blacks with gravy and pasta drips. Again, diverge'n', but in terms of grub'n', Father Antonio were a slob and my mother always lessoned me that you can judge character by table manners and that's all I'm say'n' even tho it spins future tense that she don't practice her preach'n' 'specially how it all ended so these facts is up to you to weigh.

"What can I do for you, my son?"

Father Antonio had a habit of reference'n' all the Sacred Heart dudes as son. We all detested it 'cause it were left field, but ever since my dad kicked, him call'n' me son 'eared 'ditional loon. I realized that Father Antonio were like spin'n'

some kind of spiritual father, I mean I ain't low cog, future tense I were even sit'n' classes at Beaver CC even if they were just part time classes, but low cogs don't sit no classes part time nor full. Anyway, I diverge, so back to then, when he labeled someone son, I conjured my kicked father and how I weren't his son no more.

▲▼▲

"Father, my mother told me I needed to ask you to explain something to me. She said that it weren't something a mother and a son should be discuss'n'."

Father Antonio eyed up from his cafeteria tray of green beans and tuna salad. A paper napkin hanged from his collar and bits of tuna and saliva clung to it. I 'tempted to eye his fat hands to avoid.

"Really, well what is it, my son?"

"My mother has always only hung religious stuff on the walls in our house. There's a crucifix in every room. There is prints of Jesus, Mary, and JP2 all over the place. There's a framed text of the Apostles' Creed hang'n' in the kitchen and there is several..."

"Yes son, I've been to your house. Your mother is one of the most Catholic Catholics I've ever met, but what does her decorating have to do with anything?"

"Well, there's this one thing that hangs over the mantel in the living room."

"Yes, *Christina's World*. That print was very important to your father."

"You know this? I mean everything is Jesus this and Mary that, but then there's this random print of some crippled girl stranded in a field, and you and my mother and my dad all got something 'bout it that I don't?"

Father Antonio eyed his food tray and fiddled his clerical collar and the napkin that hanged from it.

"Lots of people have prints of famous paintings hanging in their homes."

"Yeah, but when I asked my mother why, she said that my dad always wanted a girl. When I asked her what that means she said to ask you—that it were something she couldn't talk 'bout."

Father Antonio pulled the paper napkin from his collar, wadded it and dropped it into the uneaten green bean pile on the cafeteria tray. The beans were swim'n' in a cook'n' water puddle from the ladle and the napkin soaked and turned gray. It were gross like a waterlogged pretzel or a bandage afloat a public pool, but I couldn't not eye it. Father Antonio began twist'n' the emerald ring he wore on his ring finger. The ring were the size of a Super Bowl ring and it made him 'pear like a Liberace freak. Me and my group never figured why he wore it. Dudes we knowed didn't wear no jewels like that and some of us thought that maybe he were more a girl than he presented, but I'll be first to spill facts that 'side from how it spun with him and my mother, I'm thankful I never found out no porno-perv 'bout him 'cause then I'd have skyscraper problems 'top the social hooks and the trans mix that really weren't no trans mix even tho lumps keep spit'n' it. No, Father Antonio never 'tempted no porno-perv with me even tho he always wore that ring on his fat finger and that's more facts 'cause I knows some trolls are connect'n' dots and think'n' porno-perv by a priest and then girl tits and long hair and the shrunken area no wonder and that's a false facts conclusion. Real facts contra and future tense the laundry will reveal that Father Antonio were a black swan but he weren't no porno-perv black swan at least with me he weren't. The future tense facts with him and my mother is also contra to porno-perv but definite facts support'n' black swan. Maybe I can't blame my mother for it and it really hit after I rocked back to dude, but it did hit and it made it harder 'cause now they were scandal and unreliable. Digress again. Apologize and proceed.

▲▼▲

We were sit'n' in that cafeteria with green tile walls and old VCT floor tiles and the janitor we tagged Sammy Davis on 'count of his glass eye even tho who knows what his real name was, was crank'n' one of those spin'n' polishers by the food area. Father Antonio kept ring twist'n' and the napkin were now fully saturated with bean water and Father Antonio wouldn't eye at me.

"Son, this is a very delicate situation. Perhaps we should discuss this at a later time in a more private space."

"Seriously? Am I miss'n' something? I just want to know why that poster is hang'n' in my house and my mother sends me here and you tell me we better not talk about it in the cafeteria. Is it really all that?"

"Maybe not, but it is private and something better discussed in a less public space. I'll send for you this afternoon and we will discuss it in my office."

Tossed like a cow patty, I posted and told Father Antonio that I'd like that and I blew the cafeteria and Sammy Davis spin'n' his polisher 'cross the VCT.

▲ ▼ ▲

'fore Geometry and more triangles, I kicked rondo with my group, but my mind were out in space, and I couldn't co-ordinate my feet to act what my brain wanted. My group busted my balls 'bout me be'n' gimp, and so I bailed and just plopped a bench that the mouth-breathe'n' cigarette smokers commandeered for drags. There were butts all 'round the ground and I wondered why Sammy Davis weren't police'n' this mess 'stead of polish'n' the cafeteria floor for the umpteenth. I plopped in that litter till the bell and on my path to Geometry I tripped on my own feet and jammed both wrists into the mud-grass to stop from face'n'. I had green-stain-palms and no time to wash and so I popped Geometry that way and plopped the back with my paws under the desk and wrist rubbed. I did have to hit up and chalk out some junk on the board but no one were interested in the class so my group didn't eye my palms and at least I got off with that one. After class I scrubbed the stains off in the downstairs boys and then popped to Gov where we had a sub who made us do a worksheet. A little pimple freshman girl came in with a pass to free me out of there and to Father Antonio's office. The worksheet was on the government's branches and powers and controls and irrelevant facts like that, and I had no clue so I was grin'n' like a kid who just pocketed a Snickers from the 7-Eleven when I flashed the pass at the sub who were half 'sleep but 'llowed me to exit with my work incomplete.

Father Antonio was plopped 'hind a papal mahogany desk when I stepped in. There were stained glass 'hind him. One were St. Francis clam'n' a cross in one paw and a loon dove were perched on his other paw. The other window were Jesus with one paw positioned with the fingers raised and the ring touch'n' the thumb as if he were 'bout to toss a bless'n', his other paw point'n' to his glow'n' and visible sacred heart. I only knowed those windows 'cause the seven 'fore my art class walked a field trip to the office and Mrs. Ludiccino pontificated us what the windows were and this understory 'bout how they were built in Italy by some serious stain glass devotees and that the windows was boat-shipped and how everyone was fret that they might get busted but they didn't and how some special lumps installed them use'n' extreme caution and then built plexi frames inside and out for guards. I 'member that fact 'cause Mrs. Ludiccino eyed at me and my group as if we were the cause for the plexi even tho we didn't vandalize things serious. Tags with Sharpies and some practicals was 'bout how deep we cut so it were contra when Mrs. Ludiccino 'sinuated us and that's important 'cause this whole therapeutic ink is not just 'cause Therapeutic Kate specs it'll heal, it's also, and you's just learn'n' this, my contra statement and facts is facts so this is facts.

▲▼▲

Father Antonio's emerald-ringed paw motioned me to plop in one of two ancient-look'n' burgundy armchairs that furnish every church office I'd ever been in. He hit a gulp of iced coffee from a plastic tumbler and then eyed at me like my dad eyed at me when he told me the facts 'bout his cancer.

"Son, I know you've been through a lot this year. Losing a parent is one of the biggest blows anyone faces in life, but to lose a parent when you are still a young man is a combination that can lead to a knockout. You might not realize it, but you are still grieving and you probably will be for a long time to come. The grief will show in strange ways and when you least expect it, but it will show up, and you'll have to work through it with the Lord's help. Remember, the Lord will never burden us with more than we can carry."

Ever since my dad cancered and then kicked, lumps have been spout'n' me 'bout grief and the grieve'n' process, but none of it were facts to me. I 'llowed them to ramble and figured it inner-raised them to hit like all therapeutic comfort, but facts was I most didn't run on be'n' the knob whose dad kicked it. I yearned to hang with my group like past tense, but it rolled that whenever I flipped a corner there were 'nother therapeutic lump pity'n' the knob whose dad cancered. Now Therapeutic Kate is the 'ception here, but if you's crack'n' this, then maybe I laid facts incorrectly 'bout them too, but they 'structed me to ink this for therapeutic heal and it do seem to aid some so gratitude facts to you, Therapeutic Kate, for that even if you open-viewed me.

▲ ▼ ▲

I sat thru Father Antonio's pontificated theory of grief and when he kilt it, I questioned repeat 'bout the *Christina's World* that were hang'n' in the living room and my mother's nut 'bout how my dad always wanted a girl.

Father Antonio began twist'n' his emerald ring like he'd done in the cafe and he seemed to be search'n' for the right words.

"Son, I've known your parents for a long time. Did you know that I presided over their marriage?"

That's a fact everyone knowed and it were 'nother reason my group had to bust my balls. They slapped that me and Father Antonio was real bed buddies and made lots of cracks like that.

"Why, I even came to the hospital to bless you and your mother shortly after you were born."

And yes I knowed that too and facts is so did my group.

"But what your mother is referencing is the time when she was pregnant with you. You see your father started spending more and more time here in the chapel deep in prayer. I noticed, of course, but at first I just thought he was simply praying for a healthy pregnancy and a healthy child, but then your mother phoned me and said that there was something off with your father and his response to the pregnancy. She asked if I would speak with him. I agreed and one day when he was in the chapel praying, I 'proached him and asked him if he wanted to walk in the garden with me. He agreed and while we walked, he confessed to me that he was obsessed with the child his wife was carrying and obsessed with an unreasonable desire that the child be a girl. He couldn't explain it, nor could he understand it, but he was praying daily that God would grant his wish that the child would be a girl. He said it felt like if the child were a girl, she would be destined to be a saint or some revolutionary Christian in some way—that he just knowed it was meant to be. I asked him if they had seen any ultrasounds or if the doctor had told them the sex of the baby. He said that the doctor offered to tell them, but that my mother didn't want to know and that she didn't want my father to know either. She said it didn't matter if the baby were a boy or a girl—that these concerns were for the Lord to worry about. I tried to encourage your father to think about loving the baby without expectations, to love the life that the Lord was offering him, but it was no use. He couldn't stop thinking about this feeling inside him that the baby simply had to be a girl. Later when I shared this information with your mother, she said that it was characteristic of your father to get a thought in his head and then obsess over it for months."

This was facts 'bout my dad. His obsessions. Like when I were ten, my dad hooked on rehab'n' a hunt'n' cabin localed deep in the woods behind an ancient hundred acre farm close to the Allegheny River. And yep, that's the same locale that I'll get to torch'n' future tense and that lumps will say ain't a real locale, but we 'ready 'stablished it and so you's either go'n' to buy what I'm sell'n' ors you's gonna buy something else. I can't control that. All I can do is put it for sale. But diverge'n', so back to past tense facts.

▲ ▼ ▲

My dad were a realtor and land developer, and him and a few other developers had plotted to secure a hold of this old farm outside Schenley. They figured they'd install one of those everywhere subdivisions and bubble-price the abodes for Pittsburgh lumps to relocale there. Pittsburgh were start'n' to bounce from the steel crash past tense in the seventies which were when my dad were in high school so he lived those facts. The strat were that there'd be this house'n' demand and that Schenley, with its pastoral locale and the Allegheny front porch would morph into a gated village for wad-tote'n' lumps and him and his partners would be rake'n' it.

We localed in Bloomfield then and both my mother and father and all four of my grandparents was born and raised Pittsburgh. Pittsburgh roots traced to my great-grandparents—three EYE-talians and a kraut is how my dad referenced the greats. They got here like way back past tense when they was first electrify'n' light bulbs and invent'n' cars and flush toilets. My dad's kraut grandma was 'ready here when the EYE-talians moved in, and she tripped head over when she met my one great granddad at this old baseball park called Forbes. Everyone in Pittsburgh is always gush'n' 'bout Forbes and how monumental it were and like nostalgia for it as if that era were pie in the sky when it were 'round, but I'm like if it were so captain why'd they wreck'n'-ball the place to erect low-ceiling Pitt dorms?

Anyway there's this family romantic that twists that my great-grandfather eyed this kraut in the crowd, snagged a foul and gifted it to her. Most of us think this is fairytale, but my dad pretended it were facts and a sweet bio and he lit to blab it whenever newbies were 'round. My mother don't really have any tall tale 'bout her grandparents. Her grandfather just rode in on a New York train and labored the slate quarries. There ain't no Forbes Field baseball hype 'bout how he hitched my great-grandmother. They both knelt at the same EYE-talian church, met there, and coupled. Later, both my grandfathers got took on in the mills and married EYE-talian Catholic wives. But like I said, when my dad was rise'n' to high school, the steel flopped like Dumbo without ears and I spec some figured Pittsburgh were dead as a Corvair. My dad got his first hire in a paint factory but he noticed that maybe Pittsburgh were rejuvenate'n', so he took Pitt PM classes and then put the paint factory in his rearview and 'tempted to stake it in real estate deals and land development spec. He realed pretty rock at that racket, and we hauled decent bank and lived pretty fair. That Schenley subdivision notion tanked tho and him and his buds lost buckets over it. Those were some tough times for me and my mother 'cause dad were always sour and sometimes he'd Heinz 57 us. I don't think we ever lived so high after that, but we was OK and eventually he steadied and stayed ice even when he cancered.

During this time when the Schenley development was tank'n', was when my dad localed the old cabin, by this time you know what cabin I'm spill'n' 'bout, and he obsessed 'bout rehab'n' it. Maybe he RQD to divert his mind off the bank he were burn'n', who knows? But he obsessed and committed to the rehab. He halted work for seven and, with a one-man pup a few meager supplies and a trunk loaded with tools, motored the Chrysler into the woods. After that seven, he'd hit back whenever he found a day or a weekend and when it were rehabbed 'nough to bunk, he would tote me with him and sometimes him and me would Allegheny fish, but mostly him and me just labored on the cabin.

I'm spill'n' these facts 'bout origin and Pittsburgh from olden times and the cabin to 'stablish it out there and toss more contra at the opinion lumps's molded of me based on facts that ain't true. So let me 'stablish something else right now: Therapeutic Kate, all this is facts. The girl tits and the long hair and the shrunken area and the cabin and the fire and the lamb'n' of the pig. It's all facts. And if it weren't facts what else would it be. What kind of perv would imagine all this? My dad kicked, and then I grew girl tits and long hair and had to deal with the shrunken area and all that were 'gainst my wishes, and then it all reverted back to status on its own. I don't know why. It just did. I can't change that and it ain't nothing but that. There ain't no commentary on nothing like social claims there is. I'm just a dude who's 'tempt'n' to ride his life, and maybe this therapeutic ink will help in get'n' lumps off my lip and brush back the hate.

▲ ▼ ▲

I fall distracted easy and when Father Antonio were ramble'n' on 'bout grief and all, this family history sorta flooded my head. I lost some of what Father Antonio were preach'n', but I rezoned when he drew to the print.

"So then you were born and when the doctor pronounced you a boy, your father marched out of the delivery room without saying a word. Since you were a week early, you and your mother stayed in the hospital for an extra day and when it was time for the two of you to head home, miraculously your father appeared with a bouquet of flowers for your mother and a baby seat already installed in the car. He was calm and happy, and he drove you and your mother home. The strange part was though that when your mother entered the house with you in her arms, there was the framed print of *Christina's World* hanging right above the mantel where a print of da Vinci's *The Last Supper* had been. When your mother asked about the print, your father said to her that he had always wanted a girl. She never got him to explain the print other than that, and she never found out what happened to the da Vinci print. Although your father had little interest in decorating the house, the only thing he ever insisted upon was that that print remain above the mantel. Your mother decided to accept what she could not understand and learned to live with the print hanging up there. Now, after all this time, I suppose she doesn't want to take it down because it reminds her of him."

I squirmed and leaned forward in the chair.

"So you're say'n' I were a disappointment to my dad, that he didn't want me 'cause I'm a boy?"

"Now son, I would not put it that way. Your father was a good man and he cared for you and provided for your family. He grew to love you and cherish you. In fact, when he was dying in the hospital, he expressed great distress about who would be there for you as you continued to grow. He was worried that without the presence of a father, you might miss crucial guidance. No, Paul Joseph, if there was anything keeping him alive those last few months when he was truly experiencing great suffering, it was his desire to be there for you as long as he could."

"But, the *Christina's World* and my mother mute'n' me and you talk'n' to me here rather than the cafeteria? It's messed up. You say Dad didn't care short after I was born that I weren't a girl, but he made my mother keep the thing hang'n' on the wall. This is messed up."

"Son, there is a lot about life that is hard to understand. Perhaps your struggles with understanding this is part of your grief. I suggest you pray about it and place it in the hands of the Lord."

Father Antonio leaned back in his huge desk chair, and, 'hind that papal desk and in that huge chair, he looked sorta like some Mafia don, like somebody with authority that you can't do nothing 'bout.

"Now I'd say it's time for you to get back to class."

When I posted, I stumbled like an uncoordinated imbecile and almost faced. My foot must've fallen 'sleep, but I hadn't noticed it tingle'n'. I found my balance and hit back to class just as befuddled as I'd been 'fore Father Antonio's facts.

After last bell, I popped to soccer practice where I felt like I were wear'n' oversized clown shoes—I couldn't place the ball anywhere close to my targets, and I tripped twice over blades of grass. Each time my group busted my balls. After practice my coach called me over and pontificated not to fret, that I were probably in grief and that things RQD time. But I knowed this had nada to do with my dad kick'n'. I just didn't play good, that's all.

▲ ▼ ▲

My dad kick'n' were gray days, that's facts, but he was down with cancer for near three years. The hospital trips for chemo, the days he spent sprawled out on the couch pop'n' pain pills and pills that were supposed to aid thru the chemo, the revolve'n' door of gray relatives and my mother's prayer group drop'n' off casseroles and hang'n' 'round, and my mother so busy tend'n' my dad that there weren't much time left over for me. But 'fore you go and jump to conclusions and want to spec that the girl tits and long hair and shrunken area were some perv attention stunt, I'll push and spill that I didn't and don't resent my mother for tend'n' and leave'n' me to construct PB and Js when I were hungry. I got it. I knowed what was go'n' down, and I were mature 'nough to tend myself and not snuff out the candle. We had trouble 'nough with Dad's cancer. Ask anyone who's had a cancer on their couch and they'll tell you that there ain't much time to do nothing but tend. Future tense and yeah I 50% Heinz 57ed 'bout Ma and Father Antonio, but that were after the girl tits and long hair and shrunken area and I maybe wouldn't of 50% Heinz 57ed if it hadn't rendered them unlocatable and made my facts shake. But, present tense, even tho the heat keeps throw'n', nothings stick'n', but still it's harder than it should be most 'cause of the conjugal elope 'tween them, but 'gain, diverge'n'.

▲ ▼ ▲

Facts is my dad had stopped be'n' my dad long 'fore he actually kicked. When he finaled, facts is, it rocked more a feel of relief than anything. I could hit back to be'n' a regular dude, to grope'n' Jessica, to strat'n' out how to rent a prom tux, to blow'n' Saturdays mess'n' on the pitch with my group, and maybe even to cogitate'n' 'bout college and ACT scores, but facts is college and ACT scores weren't too important to me past tense and maybe eye'n' at it present tense I should've invested, but I didn't and you can't cry over spills so it is what it is and so the best I could do were part time classes at Beaver CC and anyway none of this means I ain't IQ 'nough to know the score. I know the score, believe you me. Diverge'n' 'gain. But when the cancer were full on, I just wanted what my group had—a dad that weren't kick'n' and a regular life. And that fronts me to that one deadly sin tagged envy.

Therapeutic Kate made me do a whole session 'bout envy. They pontificated it were skyscraper important and now it seems that that might be a top fact I learnt from them, that thing 'bout envy. Therapeutic Kate spilled that envy were somehow always connected to interpret'n' facts wrong. We eye some lump with polished kicks and a Beamer convertible and we cogitate that since his people is swim'n', he's all that and we eye at our rust-bucket Chevys and scuffed-up Nikes and think if-only thoughts and that's when we wash in envy. But Therapeutic Kate pontificated that we just constructed lots of 'ssumptions 'bout that lump with the polished kicks and the Beamer and we's only wash'n' envy 'bout how we think he is and not who he really is 'cause we all put our pants on one leg at a time and we all look idiotic when we's naked. It took me a while to figure that one out, 'specially the naked part 'cause when Therapeutic Kate dropped the word naked I popped other thoughts in my mind than envy. But I sees it now and facts is that Therapeutic Kate were throw'n' facts when they learnt me 'bout envy and now I know that there ain't no such thing as a regular life. We's all pack'n' skeletons and haul'n' crosses and yeah some of us haul a heftier load but we's all haul'n'. Alright, that's facts and no one likes a preacher, so I'm gonna stop spread'n' it and just say that there were no way my piss-poor athletic performance at soccer that day were grief. It were just a piss-poor athletic performance. Athletes trip them, and this were mine. I figured I RQD a boatload of protein and carbs and then a good crash, and I'd be aces at the next practice.

My mother boiled pasta and loaded it down with meat sauce for supper, and I plowed two enormous helpings, washed it down with a gob of milk, hosed off and hit the sack expect'n' all would be aces in the AM.

▲ ▼ ▲

The next day were Ash Wednesday. I woke groggy and exhausted. My chest hammered and my legs felt rubber when I peed. Twice in the bathroom I RQD to grab the vanity. It were a chill morning in the mid-forties, and in the shower I cranked the hot water full and the cold off. I were feel'n' no heat from the water that sprayed my body.

I shut the shower, dried and towel wiped fog from the mirror. At first I couldn't puzzle what hit different 'bout the reflection, but then I realized that my hair were easily an inch longer than it had been the night 'fore. It were weird, but with my hammer'n' chest and a headache, I didn't put much into sort'n' it. The hair still side-parted and combed back, so I did that and then I went to my room to dress for early Mass.

I had to plop on the bed in order to slide my legs into my khakis and not face. It were then that I eyed how red the skin on the front of my thighs was. I eyed at the skin and saw that in some places there was blisters. The shower was hotter than I had thought. You'd think the skin on my thighs be'n' all red and blisters would throb, but it didn't. I hitched up my khakis and they weren't sit'n' right but that happens and I ignored it and belted them. Ma bugged from downstairs that we had to bust and that I'd better hustle or we'd be tardy. I grabbed the school RQD oxford from my closet. I fumbled with the buttons and got the shirt closed and, feel'n' as uncoordinated as a six-foot seventh grader, I knotted the school tie 'round my neck on the third 'tempt. It were all difficult and strange, but I weren't interested in reflection. I were cogitate'n' 'bout how bore'n' Mass were go'n' to be and how I hated eye'n' all the girls with soot-smudges on their brows.

Every Ash Wednesday since I were a tyke, I had the urge to walk 'round with a wash rag and wipe the brows of Catholic girls. The soot made them look like West Virginia coal miners or dirty kids from the Hill District and that crunked me. My dad used to label me his little realist. He spilled that even when I was tyke that I'd run 'round de-mask'n' everyone on Trick-or-Treat. I never played no dress-up nor that stuff, and I specifically 'member that I wouldn't tie on this web Spiderman cape my group wanted me to sport to the school Halloween party. They all wanted to rep superheroes, but I pulled a protest and so my mother phoned me sick and I didn't go at all. There was also my tyke birthday when Aunt Polly bought me one of those plastic firefighter hats. I tantrumed when they forced it on my head for a Polaroid. Past tense I were a good tantrum thrower and once I realized that if I threw I usually got my way, it were like a nuke in my pocket—locked and loaded and ready to blow whenever RQD. I guess I stopped that 'round ten or so when Jimmy V called me a flower when he eyed me toss'n' a tantrum when my mother wouldn't let me skip a First Friday to go to a Pirates game for Shrimp's birthday. Anyway, I didn't and I don't costume and that's more facts that I weren't play'n' at be'n' a girl. I were a girl for a while. Well Tessie said I weren't, but I did have girl tits and long hair and that shrunken area, but it weren't a costume and I didn't choose it nor want it. It just was what it was and then it went away. That's it. But 'nother thing that I sometimes think 'bout now is that maybe that was why the *Christina's World* print bothered me so much—it weren't rep'n' my mother, it were false and contra. My mother was, as Father Anonio proclaimed her, a very Catholic Catholic. At least that is what I figured at the time and mostly I guess still do but the couple'n' stuff future tense is a bit contra to that, but I already spilled the facts on that so I probably should zip that for now.

▲ ▼ ▲

In the Chrysler to church, I started cogitate'n' 'bout soccer and that if I really were ill my moves would slip and I might even drop my start. Josh Baccio was better than I wanted him to be and wouldn't it be my luck to drop my spot to a sophomore. I started feel'n' all fret that if I had 'nother piss-poor practice, he'd usurp and supersede me. I certainly weren't feel'n' aces. I didn't know what were happen'n' with me or my body, but the last thing' I RQD was some sophomore usurp'n' me like I did to Clayton Thomas who used to start till I slid 'head. He weren't overjoyed 'bout it neither and even picked with me outside the lockers, but not only was I better on the pitch I were also better with my hands. After that he had a bench seat and a blood nose. 'fore you go and 'gain start psychologize'n' and all theorize'n', let's 'stablish more facts. I ain't violent, and I don't go 'round crunch'n' noses. Clayton came at me 'cause he were sore 'bout his spot and yeah I'm chippy on the pitch and yeah I'm gonna stick up for myself like my dad stuck up for himself, but I don't go look'n' for it. The pig got what he got 'cause he came full porno-perv at me. I were mind'n' my own and work'n' things out and he came at me. Maybe I did lamb him, but it were defense and even tho present tense I'm a person of interest whenever the heat finds a lambed home-less lump, facts is nothing sticks 'cause the heat knows it were defense and there weren't really no evidence 'cept the pig be'n' miss'n' and last seen in those woods by where the cabin that lumps claim ain't was and even tho they never found Jessup or Tumult or even Tessie, the heat had nothing to lead on but me spill'n' I lambed a pig 'cause I tells facts, mostly always have, and pin'n' me just for be'n' a boy-girl delinquent were stretch'n' and eventually the judge had to see that even if I did it like I creeded I did it, I were duressed. Facts is facts and the way-far-outers who use so-cial to conjure a drag serial are as wack as the ones who claim government pedos which don't make no sense neither. A drag serial. Please? But here I am diverge'n' and I was try'n' to tell this chronological. We'll get to that stuff. You RQ background to line up the facts right.

▲ ▼ ▲

Mass was as boring as a block of yellow cheese, and I couldn't keep my eyes from shut'n'. I even RQD to plop when everyone stood and I leant my butt on the bench during the kneel'n' even tho it were something tykes and grandmothers did. My mother RQD to bump me to go receive ashes. I leaned on the end of pews as I managed the line toward Fa-ther Antonio who posted in front of the communion rail hold'n' a silver bowl of soot and smear'n' foreheads with his fat greasy thumb. When I got to him, Father Antonio had to push my bangs back off my forehead 'fore he could mark soot on my brow.

"Son, remember you are dust and to dust you shall return."

Even tho I usually didn't think all that much 'bout my father at the time, Father Antonio's creepy words flashed an image in my head of my father morph'n' to dust. When I managed back to the pew and plopped my seat, I thought of my father live'n' in the casket but down underground and I sorta wanted to get a spade or pick and go to his grave and disinter him up just for certain's sake. I'd had that inkle'n' once or twice in the ago and once I dreamt it and in that dream I begged lumps to disinter him up 'cause I were in a wheelchair unbeknownst, but everyone were vacuum'n' or jog'n' and no lump would bother. That obviously weren't a good dream.

▲▼▲

After Mass, Mother whispered to Father Antonio who marked an extra smudge of palm soot on her forehead. They hugged 'fore she maneuvered into the Chrysler and drove 'way with a wave and a horn toot. I already 'stablished that we ain't further divert'n' here. This is 'bout my girl tits and long hair and shrunken area and that's 'bout something else and that something else ain't something I'm curious to reprise present tense.

▲▼▲

I stayed for school even tho my chest was throbs and it was struggles to walk in some fashion that didn't make me 'pear like a drunk flower. I managed to the cafeteria for a cream cheese bagel and chocolate milk. The cafeteria lady flashed when she charged my credit.

"You're lucky you're still young enough to be allowed to eat today. Just between you and me, fasting really sucks."

She winked and dropped a ham and egg on my tray.

"This one's on me. A growing boy needs to eat."

I rocked some energy after I grubbed and made it thru the AM with just a bloat pain in my pecks which was strange 'cause I ain't pumped a chest-day since that past Friday. At lunch, Jessica bugged to know what were up with my hair.

"Nothing, it's just my hair."

I slid my tray 'cross from hers and plopped a seat.

Jessica and I hooked at fall homecome'n', and we'd been steady since. I had spilled to my group that we copulated and sometimes I'd even spill them stuff 'bout Jessica's tits but I usually felt bad 'bout that and I think everyone knew I were misrepresent'n' 'cause Jessica's rep were conserve in that department and her group were conserve too. There's the other group that's the opposite, but at that time I hain't never been with no one from that group so I'd just sometimes spread up that me and Jessica were hit'n' even tho it weren't facts. This ain't evidence that the other stuff's a lie. It's contra that when I lie I admits the lie and so if that other stuff were a lie I'd admit it too but I ain't admit'n' it so it's facts and that's that.

The facts is Jessica was a virgin, and we pressed a lot but that's 'bout it. She were the captain of the basketball team and a lightn'n' sprinter in track. Since we was both athletes, her and me connected and hyped to train together and be all her versus me all the time. She wore her hair short and when she wasn't wear'n' the RQD plaid skirt and white pullover, she only wore athletic stuff and Nikes. She didn't look spec in the school uni but in athletic clothes she was smoke.

"Your hair, it looks different, longer or something."

The palm soot smudged on Jessica's brow distracted, and I eyed it like those movie psychos who have to stare at ink blots in some Dr. Freud office.

"Maybe it's just these stupid ashes. We's all walk'n' freaks like this. If ETs come right now they'd think we's pretty weird."

"I don't think it's about the ashes. It's like your hair grew a lot longer overnight. It wasn't anywhere near that long yesterday."

She reached 'cross the table and fingered my bangs down 'cross my face. They reached the tip of my nose.

"See, your hair's really long all of the sudden."

I was absent for words. It were facts that yesterday if I brushed my hair toward it would have barely reached my eyes and now it were on the tip of my nose. I had no explanation and things was elaborated by my pressurized chest. It were like my ribs were break'n' from the inside out or something. It weren't like push'n' in, it was push'n' out like a tire that you pump PSI up way past recs and that's something you don't know unless by experience. You might think you know, but think that a balloon is in your chest and it starts to blow up inside there and there's nowhere for it to go so it pushes your ribs out and you'd sorta get the feel.

▲ ▼ ▲

To divert, I bit into my chicken patty and ran on with my mouth full even tho it weren't manners and I knowed it.

"It's always been this long, I just keep it combed back. Maybe you should pay more attention to how your guy looks."

I swallowed and flashed my teeth. Jessica kicked my smile.

"I know how you look, and I know your hair wasn't like this yesterday. Did you have some sort of growth spurt or something? Are you taller also?"

"No, I'm still five-eleven as far as I knows. What 'bout you? You have a growth spurt?"

"Why would you ask that? I'm not the one with the hair."

"I don't know. Maybe I don't want to talk about my hair. I'm not feel'n' aces, and I got soccer practice. I was a total waste yesterday and now I feel like a puddle of mud. I'm reasonably sure that I'm gonna crap all over myself 'gain today. So I ain't too curious 'bout my hair if you catch what I'm throw'n'."

Jessica caught it but weren't too happy. She didn't rock when I stopped a flow. She postulated that I's king of redirect from things I don't want to spill 'bout and that it's annoy'n'. She creeded something she learnt in English 'bout spontaneous text'n' or something like that. She bought into it be'n' rock and were always 'tempt'n' to conversate spontaneous and all ramble. She creeded it were to expand and liberate. She learnt that from the hippie who taught English to the APs. I weren't an AP, but we all knowed the hippie 'cause she were all tie-dye and braids and Birks and no one else rocked that. My group couldn't figure what she were do'n' there, but she were there right next to the sisters and fathers and it were contrast like porno-Disney. Future tense and she drifted on, but while the girl tits and long hair and shrunken area was happen'n' she were there. Digress. I'm try'n'. Sorry.

▲▼▲

We ate as much of the chicken patties as we could stand and used the soggy fries to scoop ketchup. I had two chocolate milks but still dropped my tray 'fore get'n' to the window. It clanged, and lumps gawked and blew milk. I didn't red it but just left the mess for Sammy Davis and stepped outside for rays before the bell. I'd probably get a detention for blind-eye'n' the mess, but I wasn't go'n' to red that up in front of a bunch of pimples and frosh. Now I'm go'n' to divert intentionally 'cause you RQ to know 'bout that tray drop 'cause it shows that I'm spill'n' the entire not just what I wants you to know and by spill'n' the entire I sometimes got to spill the bad with the good. I ain't hip to snitch'n' on me but if you know the bad and the good my cred is up and facts are facts.

▲ ▼ ▲

After more triangle pontification, the bell rung and I changed into gear and went to practice. Immediately Jimmy V blasted a rocket into my chest and I crumpled. In and off season, I was a regular in the weight room and even tho my group busted my balls 'bout it, I toned on my upper as well as my legs. Result was I had a six and rock pecs and looked sweet poolside, yet the missile to my chest drove nails. I rolled to and fro on the ground like a girl and my long hair in my face were the only thing that stopped my tears from show'n' and that were fortuitous 'cause I'd never recover rep if my group eyed me bawl'n' like a five year old girl. The trainer got two jvs to assist me to my feet and I draped off the pitch and into the train'n' room. I climbed on the padded table and when the jvs left, I pulled off my jersey so the trainer could examine. When he poked for broken ribs, we were both surprised by flesh and bloat which the trainer theorized were on 'count of the missile shot. He prescribed me to chill and ice and charted the no-go on continue'n'. I passed the rest of the practice bench'n' with ice Saraned to my chest.

After that, I tripped like a senile grandmother and slapped hard into the first row of gray bleachers. Other than trip'n' and bust'n' open the ice all over the place, I seemed uninjured and pulled myself back to my feet and began walk'n' toward the stadium exit where my mother was idle'n' the Chrysler. When I climbed in she freaked.

"What in the world happened to your arm?"

"Nothing happened to my arm, I took a ball to the chest, that's all."

"No, your arm? Why, it's cut to the bone. You're bleeding all over the place."

My mother grabbed a blanket from the back and tried to staunch the bleed. She told me to press it firm 'gainst the gash and that we RQD to bust it to the ER.

"That's going to need stitches in the best case scenario. Let's hope it's not worse."

"Ma, it's just a little cut. It don't hurt."

My mother geared the Chrysler out into the street and maneuvered toward St Luke's.

"Don't play brave for me, I know it's got to be killing you. My gosh, you're just like your father, always stoic—the silent suffering type."

At the ER, I were triaged quick. The blanket I was firm'n' 'gainst my arm was drop'n' red, and I were so dazed that I RQD to post on my mother to make it from the Chrysler to the doors. A large woman in hip hop jeans and an aqua scrub shirt materialized with a wheelchair and aided. She pushed me into the treatment area and this smoke doc in maroon scrubs and examination gloves eyed at me. I didn't pay attention when she told her name. I were dizzy and I were distracted by how smoke she was. She didn't scan older than me and she had short hair like Jessica's. She had the body of a runner and I hoped I weren't show'n' nothing embarrass'n', but, if I were, she weren't look'n' 'cause she peeled the blanket and whistled.

"Wow, that's a deep cut there. How'd you do that?"

"I fell, I guess. I didn't know I did it till my mother pointed it. It ain't nothing."

The smoke doc raised brows. Her forehead furrowed like a rippled sand dune and I eyed lines around her eyes. She were older than scanned, but she were still smoke and I rocked look'n' at her green eyes. Drift'n', I played forward if Jessica would still smoke and then played get'n' with someone like the smoke doctor—past tense of high school, maybe past tense of college.

"You gashed your upper arm down to the bone and you didn't know you did it? Come on, it has to hurt like hell. On a scale of one to ten, how would you rate your pain?"

I glanced her badge. Addy Madison, M.D. I played walk'n' it with Addy Madison, M.D. and how her and me would be balls to my group and how she'd pride to her group 'bout me be'n' a soccer stud and in high for MVP and could have been captain if I took it but that I pity-deferred to Jimmy V 'cause he's a last year. I was spin'n' and trip'n' and all distraction and mind play'n'.

Addy Madison, M.D. crouched down in front of me and eyed dead into my eyes.

"Paul Joseph, you've lost a lot of blood and you're fading in and out. Try to look at me and focus. On a scale of one to ten, how would you rate your pain?"

I deeped into Addy Madison, M.D.'s greens and flashed Jessica's face then my mother's then Father Antonio's then Addy Madison, M.D.'s 'gain.

"Take a deep breath and focus."

I gulped oxygen and kinda got panic and suffocated. My chest racked when I sucked in air. Like a hyperventilated baby, I lost my breath'n' rhythm but still played Addy Madison, M.D. as my arm and flash worried 'bout rotten breath.

"Close your mouth and breathe through your nose."

Addy Madison, M.D.'s examination-gloved finger pushed one of my nostrils closed.

"Now focus, Paul Joseph, focus. You've gotten yourself all worked up. Focus and slow breathing. That's it. Don't inhale or exhale too quickly. Just slow calm inhales and exhales. That's it."

Addy Madison, M.D.'s other hand clammed mine. When I restarted my rhythm, Addy Madison, M.D. released my nostril and slipped out of my hand.

"Now Paul Joseph, you've got to focus here. On a scale of one to ten, how much pain are you in?"

"My chest hurts."

Addy Madison, M.D. placed her palms on my knees and reengaged eye to eye.

"You don't have to play the tough guy for me, Paul Joseph. I see all kinds of people injured in all kinds of ways. Pain is normal and nothing to be embarrassed about. I just need to know where you are so I can help you feel better. On a scale of one to ten, can you rate your pain?"

I specced 'bout my arm and it were absent. I glanced to make sure it existed and then I eyed back at Addy Madison, M.D. Man, she was smoke.

"It really don't hurt."

"Paul Joseph, you answer the doctor right this instant."

I had forgot my mother and then me show'n' for Addy Madison, M.D. grossed me.

"My chest hurts is all."

Addy Madison, M.D. called for a nurse and after half an hour I were sutured, bandaged and slung. Addy Madison, M.D. diagnosed the wound as deep and I had internal and external sew'n'.

I were still dizzy and my chest were rack'n' like stallions was kick'n' escape. Mother revealed that they told her I'd lost a decent drop of blood and that's why I were dizzy. Hip hop jeans rematerialized and worked me back to a wheelchair. My mother posted 'side me and assured Addy Madison, M.D. that she would be sure to make an appointment with our family doc for a follow. But 'fore hip hop jeans ran the chair out, Addy Madison, M.D. cleared her throat.

"You are Paul Joseph's mother, correct?"

My mother acknowledged. She still had palm soot smudged on her brow and I was in touch with not want'n' Addy Madison, M.D. to eye that on her or me.

"Well, there's something else."

Addy Madison, M.D. was scrub'n' her hands and spill'n' into the sink.

"Your son says he didn't feel any pain when he injured his arm, and I barely gave him any lidocaine when I stitched up his wound. I expected him to wince or something to indicate that he really was in pain and then I was planning on giving him a full dose, but he didn't even seem to notice the suturing. In fact, it was like it wasn't even happening to him."

"Well, he's a lot like his father. Neither one likes to show any weakness. I watched his father fight cancer with ibuprofen for over a year and a half before accepting anything stronger. Paul Joseph takes after him."

Addy Madison, M.D. fronted. Her greens sparked and her whites glistened.

"Be that as it may, I think it is best that we keep Paul Joseph here and test him for drug use."

My mother clutched her purse and made the sign of the cross.

"Drug use? You can't be serious."

Addy Madison, M.D. touched my mother's upper arm.

"I can imagine how hard it is to hear this, but a major laceration that Paul Joseph didn't even notice, general numbness and dizziness. The hyperventilating and drifting in and out of lucidity. There are a lot of red flags here. With the current opioid epidemic, I think it would be wise to check."

My mother eyed at me as if for the first time in her life she thought Paul and Joseph were now in cahoots with Judas. Then faith kicked and she sided with me.

"Opioids? Are you crazy? This is my son. He's a good student and an athlete. He would never do something like that."

While I 'eared, the scene shifted to movie and actors vers'n' over something other than me. My body lifted in space, and I was locked. My mouth couldn't sound. When my mother bent down to eye me in the eyes and hit me point blank if I were on drugs. I was ice and out of shout'n' range. I weren't if that's what you're think'n'. What went down weren't drugs and that's more facts for the case. One time Jimmy V hit a roid he secured from his uncle who was a gym rat, but he reported it made him regurgitate and have the shits simultaneous and that was the end of that. Other than that roid, my group weeded limited and nixed true rock in favor of athletics. Jessica weren't into it neither so other than weed'n' light and Jimmy V's roid fail, Addy Madison, M.D.'s 'cusation falsified. Prisoned inside my body like a loon in a strait-jacket, my silence was consent and my mother's disappointment was a beached whale.

Addy Madison, M.D. touched my shoulder which didn't spark me none 'cause her smoke were dissipated. If she was look'n' to boogie, she was 'bout to get the shake.

"I'm sorry, Mrs. Rizzo but look, Paul Joseph can't even speak. I'm not saying he's definitely on drugs, but something is off and ruling out drug use is the logical first step to figuring out what is going on."

I lifted to spar with Addy Madison, M.D., but only inched and plopped back with dizzy fret that my jacket was misbuttoned but facts were that I weren't wear'n' no jacket. I lifted 'gain with more progress but soon hit limp and, like a timbered tree, tilted forward out the wheelchair and face planted the tile floor. The next thing I's regain'n' in a hospital bed in a semi-private and my mother is fret 'side me pray'n' her Rosary. My chest tendered and sored and, as if I were hide'n' in the weeds, it was difficult to clear. I realized that my difficulty was hair over my eyes. I reach up to finger it back. It was at least a foot long and the sheer volume of hair on my head was shock. My mother was weep'n' as she prayed with her eyes closed. She mouthed the Hail Marys. I reached over and gentle-touched her hand to 'lert I were 'wake.

She opened her eyes and eyed at me like I were an outed Barney the Purple Dinosaur.

"Paul Joseph, what have you done?"

Now this is where you need to see facts. See this is the moment when the girl tits and the hair and the shrunken area come in and if I spun the lead-up right, you can jump to I ain't done nothing to invite this and when my mother 'cuses what I was pull'n', it's obvious that I weren't. Contra to denial tho, I muted myself and puzzled her. My mother questioned me second.

My throat were dry and scratchy like sandpaper and sawdust. I yearned for some agua. Mother poured some plus ice into a plastic cup, put a flex straw in the cup and held it to my lips. The agua were cool and refresh and, but for the vice grips in my chest, I was register'n' regular—not aces but at least queens, maybe even kings.

"Ma, I ain't."

"You just need to rest. You're in St. Luke's and the doctors are trying to piece together what's happening to you. They think you took some drugs laced with estrogen and maybe some anesthetizing agent. How could you be so stupid? Paul Joseph, I know your father died and you are grieving, but to turn to drugs. I just don't understand it. May God have mercy on you. My son, the drug addict. I never thought I'd say those words."

My mother bowed and wept. She clutched the Rosary and rocked back and forth.

"Ma, I ain't on nothing. What are you talk'n' 'bout?"

She eyed with tears.

"I've asked Father Antonio to visit and speak with you. I honestly don't know what to do. First your father's cancer and now you with the drugs. The Lord really does work in mysterious ways."

I 'tempted up. Just my head lifted. Nothing else. I asked my mother to lift the head of the bed. She fiddled with rail'n' buttons and eventually raised me to semi-sit'n'. I reached for her hand and she clammed my palm. Typically my mother's cold. Past tense those hands freshed me. When I would bust upset, or skid a scrape or general go blue, her cool hands would caress and assure. Something was foul 'cause in that semi-private, her hands were absent. I comprehended that we were clammed, but I couldn't weigh, temperature, or tight the grip. Perhaps an asleep hand yet no tingles so the facts were that I stumped it, but 'fore I could figure, there were moans from the other side of the curtain and commotion and regurgitate noises and tussle noises even cop noises. When settlement happened, I 'eared my mother whimper.

"Ma, I ain't. I ain't"

"Then how do you explain those?"

My mother's hand pulled from mine and her finger directed to my chest. I eyed down, and, here's the facts that I can't explain but right there where past tense solid pecs were were now present tense twin grapefruit breasts and that's the first time I popped girl tits and it weren't for any reason that I knowed.

▲▼▲

I were as confused as a neanderthal figure'n' algebra. Two obvious girl tits were set'n' right there under my hospital gown. I cupped them and experienced a sort of simultaneous pleasure and pain. The tits themselves were tender and sore and they pained when I touched them; yet, my hands were feel'n' when Jessica allowed me to fondle. I reddened and fast uncupped my girl tits. My mother was eye'n' me fondle myself. These girl tits were certainly attached to me, and I should have felt as natural touch'n' them as I felt scratch'n' my nose or wash'n' myself down there, but somehow it felt foul and porno-perv to touch them while my mother was plop'n' right there 'side me.

My mind was spin'n' like a bent corner kick. I eyed at my mother and her smear mascara and knowed that she'd been bawl'n' like a busted lawn sprinkler. She clammed my hand and wrapped the rosary 'round it.

"Paul Joseph, we need to know what you took. This is not a game. The Lord only knows what else is going to happen to your body."

She spilled slow and purpose and annunciated every syllable. She hit the 'cent on the end of every word, which were her habit when she was spray'n' something she creeded important. I 'membered when she hit me with my father's palliative. *It is mere-lée a mat-tér of ti-íme, Pa-úl Jo-séph.*

I reclaimed my hand and pointed.

"Ma, what's happen'n'? Why are you cry'n'? Why are you so serious? What drugs? What's go'n' on?"

"Pa-úl Jo-séph, you nee-eéd to tell us a-bóut the dru-úgs."

I combed my fingers thru long thick hair, grabbed a handful, and lifted straight 'bove my head to display its length.

"Ma, I have no idea what's go'n' on. I got blasted with a soccer ball and then I gashed my arm and now I'm here in this bed with girl tits and long hair."

My mother winced at the word tits, and I rephrased to breasts.

More commotion came from the other side of the curtain and machinery was carted in and many personnel in scrubs crowded. Beeps and stats and a verbal front between a cop and a nurse 'bout transfer to lockdown and when the smoke cleared they filed out and two men emerged and pushed a bed with a restrained gnarly skeleton tied tight and all 'struggle.

"He's a junky, Paul Joseph. He's a junky. You're on a drug ward. Lord, a drug ward."

"I ain't, Ma. I ain't."

"You are not what, Paul Joseph? A druggy? A junky? Well what else are we supposed to conclude?"

My mother fell to mumble'n' Hail Marys and finger'n' her Rosary.

I slipped out and when I came back, my mother were changed into a clean blouse and her makeup were reapplied. She still clutched the Rosary, but she composed better. When she eyed that I were back, she clammed my hand and whispered into my ear.

"Pa-úl Jo-séph, I know that you know about the changes to your body but there is some-thíng ell-élse, but Fa-thér An-to-ni-ó is go-íng to have to dis-cúss it with you-ú."

"What else could there be, Ma? I don't think it can get no worse than this."

It was then that it 'curred. If my hair... if two decent girl tits... my hand reached under the blanket. I gasped. Everything down there were miniature like what a baby might have. And facts is that I ain't too into spill'n' 'bout that embarrassment 'cause even tho the girl tits and hair eventually dissipated, there's those who spec that the down there ain't come back. Facts is that it has even tho social reports that that don't come back when you reverse. But Google it and slide past the porno-perv that hits first and you'll see on M.D. sites that it comes back upon reversal. But regards, you can imagine lose'n' it and even gain'n' girl tits ain't worth lose'n' that.

"What's happen'n' to me?"

I ain't a pray person and especially now after all this I ain't a pray person, but when I realized the shrunk mini, my free hand made the sign of the cross. I had largely dropped on God past tense my father's cancer, but whatever purpose he served evaporated totally as I eyed my father, a solid man, a stone dad, and a relative youth, wither 'way like a stick of butter in a fry pan. My mother and her prayer group circle'n' and recite'n' we-implore-the-aid-of-tender-mercy BS. There weren't no intervention just silence. Silence is all it ever were. This YouTube demonstrated that there's noise in the universe that we can't 'ear 'cause we ain't listen'n' close 'nough. That might be facts, but it ain't no God commotion. God don't talk. I knowed that, yet, desperate times. I crossed myself and started bargain'n'. I dealt the bastard that I'd be better, that I'd rock church, that I'd pray continuously, that I'd even maybe be a priest if only I'd get my shrunken area restored.

Tears welled and soon I were bawl'n' 'gain like a little girl. I frustrated and confused. My mother comforted, but she had no explanation other than drug use which were a stab in the dark. Facts 'ready 'stablished there. Estrogen? Maybe the girl tits but the hair? Estrogen don't grow no hair like that.

Quietly, Father Antonio entered the semi-private. He handed my mother on the shoulder to 'lert her. My mother released and leaned back. I eyed thru tears and blanketed the girl tits. My mother stood and walked. She spilled that Father Antonio were prep'n' prayer. I stifled and nodded. She hugged Father Antonio, for too long if facts is tell'n' 'specially with revelation, but I weren't think'n' that then. Father Antonio plopped where my mother vacated and with his hands clasped leaned in.

"Son, it seems you've gotten yourself in quite a pickle."

I always riled corny spews like *in a pickle, shame on me,* and *it's a real hoot.* They all seem so octogenarian that I never figured how anyone lower than a hundred could spit them and not feel ass dumb.

"Father, I don't know what's go'n' on."

"Son, I think you do."

I eyed Father Antonio. His clerical collar were not fastened correctly and part of it were loose from the slot. It were like one of those old time comics with a shirt collar that springs open. I weren't 'bout to revelate 'bout an awry collar if he were plop'n' 'cusations.

"You think I do? You think I do what, Father?"

"I think you know exactly what's happening to you. After all your poor mother has been through, to go and pull this little stunt is truly shameful. You are lucky that the Lord is a compassionate lord. You should be ashamed of yourself."

"I ain't done nothing."

"Not done anything? Are you seriously telling me that? You have all but driven the last nail in your mother's coffin with this stunt."

"Stunt?"

"Do you have a better word for it? Antic? Foolhardy? Silliness? Maybe you and your friends think games like these are funny, but they are not. It is a blessing that your father is not around to see what you have gone and done."

Spit'n' 'bout my father were a low blow. I had not done nothing. What were Father Antonio spread'n'? Did he conjure I were stag'n'? That I had concocted out some 'laborate scheme to illusion that I were a girl? Why on Earth would I play that? I went 50% Heinz 57 and probs would have popped 100% if I weren't still experience'n' some grogginess.

"Father, I ain't."

"Son, denial is not the way to forgiveness. The sooner you take responsibility and truly repent your evil ways, the sooner we can all start to heal from the hurt you've caused."

I reached 'cross for the plastic cup of ice water on the side table. My arm hit 'gainst my new girl tits. I'd momentary forgot these, and I were jarred and flipped the cup. Water and ice spilled on Father Antonio's pant leg. Father Antonio leapt. He impulsively brushed the wet. His face were as red as a dog tongue.

"My God son, what is wrong with you? Don't you realize we are here to help you? Is this how you treat people?"

Father Antonio 'treated to the bathroom, yanked paper towel from the dispenser and sopped his trousers.

"Look son, I'm really trying to be understanding here. I know you are grieving, but think about the people you are hurting. Is this how you want to treat people?"

Here were the repeat. Psychologize that I were grieve'n'. Facts is that I weren't grieve'n', and even if, how would that explain girl tits and long hair and a shrunken area? Kindle was spark'n' and I reddened like 75% Heinz 57.

"Son, did you get the drugs at school? I need to know. You can be honest with me. If we have a dealer at Sacred Heart, I need to know. We can't let this happen to others. Even if you don't care how this affects you or your poor mother, at least consider how it will impact your friends."

"Father Antonio, I ain't do'n' no drugs."

I spit the words and fisted my hands.

Bits of wet paper clung to the black fabric of Father Antonio's pant leg. The remains of saturated paper he dropped in the trash. He walked to the small counter by the door where he had stowed a bag of his hospital visit paraphernalia. He palmed an ancient look'n' leather bound prayer book. He thumbed it. There were soot ground in his thumb. He didn't wash good which is gross and 'nother reason that he were alien. He lifted one hand in a heil Hitler.

"God, by the means of dumb animals You have given help to men in their labors. We humbly beg of You that these animals, without which our human wants cannot be supplied, be not lost to our use, through Christ our Lord."

He eyed at me.

"This is where you say amen, son"

I mumbled it.

"We humbly beg of You, Lord, in Your mercy, that in Your name and by the power of Your blessing, You cure this animal afflicted with a serious disease. May all power of the devil that is in him be driven out. And that he be not any more afflicted by disease, Lord, be for him a guard of his life and remedy producing health, through Jesus Christ Your Son, our Lord, who lives and is King and God with You in the unity of the Holy Spirit for ever and ever."

Still with his heil, Father Antonio eyed at me.

"Hmmmm..."

"Amen."

I mumbled as I eye-daggered Father Antonio.

He lowered his heil.

"Son, do you know what I just recited?"

I shook head.

"I just recited the prayer for a suffering animal. Now you might wonder why I would do something like that. Well, son, you see you are not acting human. Something has gotten a hold of you, and you are now acting animalistic. We need to break this animal cycle and return you to a compassionate and loving human being—one who can care for your mother, stop hurting others and respect the body the Lord gave you. Until you drive out the beast that has taken hold of you, there is no hope."

I eye-daggered Father Antonio like he were a drunk peg-leg sailor. This were out of pocket. This had to be hallucination.

A nurse knocked. She were older and eyed like she should be Lazy-Boy'n' it with baked cookies and manicured geraniums. She vitaled me and offered food which I snubbed. Facts was that I were always hungry past tense and took in grub like a garbage truck but in the semi-private, I weren't not hungry nor hungry. She palmed my shoulder and claimed that she were a helper. Alls I needed to do was push the call button, and she'd magically appear. She fingered back my hair and spilled that I twinned her granddaughter. She cleared. Father Antonio eyed like he had just witnessed a school bus truck'n' 'cross the surface of Lake Erie.

"Son, has it really gone this far? Why would you allow her to believe you are a girl?"

It was when Father Antonio spewed that—believe you are a girl— that I figured it. *Christina's World* and my mother spew'n' 'bout my father.

"Father, is this connected with *Christina's World*?"

"Connected with *Christina's World*? Are those drugs melting your brain? You really think you can dismiss this as some supernatural phenomenon just because one time, many years ago, your father had a moment? Please. You did this to yourself, and you're soon going to learn that this is a poor way to get attention. The sooner you own up to the beast that has a hold of you, the sooner the Lord will help you defeat the beast."

I was full Heinz 57 and spit while I spewed.

"You said my father always wanted a girl, and now I'm change'n'."

"Son, you will not take that tone of voice with me. Let's calm yourself down and think about what you just said. Do you really think that just because someone wants something, that poof it happens? If that were true, everyone would have a million dollars and happy lives. The world does not work like that. The Lord does not work like that. I don't understand why you won't come clean and admit that you've been taking drugs. The evidence is undeniable. There is no other explanation. And to think about the other students at Sacred Heart who are also in danger of this happening to them. Son, you are being selfish. If you won't save yourself, don't take others down with you. Who is the dealer? How many kids are using? How big is this problem in the high school?"

There were Sacred Heart lumps who weeded heavy and a few who I 'eared were mess'n' with the real, but poppers at Sacred Heart were minimal. Present tense, social don't creed it when I spill it, yet I'll establish facts repeat umpteenth that I weren't rock'n' nothing. Everyone seemed and seems to conjure I were. 'sides, even if I were, who ever noted morph'n' gender via weed? Populus weed'n' ongo'n' and as far as I knows, none of them is morph'n' gender. Father Antonio were relentless. He grimy-thumbed prayer book pages, localed what he were dig'n', and 'gain heil Hitlered.

"Pray with me, son."

I dogged my head and lowered lids.

"God of life, You made Paul Joseph in Your perfect image, to live in Your love and to give You glory, honor and praise. Open his heart to Your healing power. Come, Lord Jesus, calm Paul Joseph's soul just as you whispered 'Peace' to the stormy sea.

"St. Jude, most holy Apostle, in Paul Joseph's need we reach out to you. I beg you to intercede for him that he may find strength to overcome his illness. Bless all those who struggle with addiction. Touch them, heal them, reassure them of the Father's constant love. Remain at Paul Joseph's side, St. Jude, to chase away all evil temptations, fears, and doubts. May the quiet assurance of your loving presence illuminate the darkness in Paul Joseph's heart and bring lasting peace."

Father Antonio silenced. I eyed him. He statued the heil.

"Hmmmm..."

"What? You want me to say Amen? Amen, there I said it. Does that make me not a girl no more?"

I were really Heinz 57.

Father Antonio lowered the heil and shut the prayer book. He looked like a volcano spit'n' ash and 'bout to lava.

"Son, the Lord helps those who help themselves. I can do nothing else for you or sadly for your mother until you are willing to take responsibility for what you have done. May

God have mercy on you, Paul Joseph, may God have mercy on you."

Turn'n' toward the door, Father Antonio stopped to stow his prayer book in his satchel, slid into the shoulder strap and marched out.

I were relieved. It were like the referee had TKOed the bout. I palmed my girl tits 'gain. Altho I porno-perved them, they were sore and tender. I deferred to rather rid the bed and glance my reflection.

The safety rails were locked in the up, sos climb'n' out were complicated. To further, my legs were numb and once I maneuvered myself to the foot of the bed and 'tempted to post, I lost balance and plopped back on the mattress. I figged I RQD to readjust and that I must have been on that mattress for seven for my hair to sprout so long and these girl tits to appear, not to mention whatever was go'n' on down there. As I re'tempted to post, I slowed and palmed the rail. Focus'n' on steady, I forged my way to the bathroom door mirror. Facts is that I weren't certain I wanted to eye when I maneuvered in position to reflect, but I knowed I RQD to eye it 'cause it ain't no use live'n' in denial. Face facts. That's that. Sos when I reflected a smoke girl I spun to see who's behind. Thus, I lost balance and crashed. I grabbed the paper towel dispenser and carried it down with me. I weren't hurt and slowed to my feet and reposted the reflection. This time no shock 'cause I knowed the smoke girl were me. I was definitely smoke and facts were that I were crush'n' right there and that's one of those things that I don't like to admit but facts is that throw'n' truth, good and bad, is how cred is built so there is the bad. I could've porno-perved myself if the sitch were a bit altered. That's abnormal facts to admit, but there it is. My stone athletic were vanished. In place of my ripped arms were the appendages of Jessica. I were still stone, but girl stone. Like less ripple and increase curve. Definitely smoke to eye at if I disassociated the reflection, but when real, disorient'n'. My legs emerge'n' from the hospital gown were leaner which made them look elonged.

The gown hung like a dress which completed the transformation.

Future tense at Beaver CC, I cracked Kafka's *The Metamorphosis*. See facts: I ain't low cog. I cogitated that Gregor were able to stow in his room when he transformed. I were a flimsy gown away from be'n' naked and displayed in a semiprivate. All I yearned was to seclude to my bedroom, lock the door and figure what were happen'n'. I RQD solitude. I didn't want Father Antonio's badgers 'bout grief and drugs and heil-recite'n' old prayers. I didn't want my mother camp'n' out in front of me all weep and Rosary. I RQD solitude. Facts is I still do. Social never sleeps so you can forget 'bout that tho. I see now, Therapeutic Kate, what you was hit'n' when you suggested I ghost social. You theorized that social weren't no friend to most lumps and that it were 'specially not no friend to me. No, social never sleeps. Like I spilled, present tense, I get that, but then I weren't cogitate'n' 'bout social, I were stuck on the reflect of my girl body and sorta lost in myself till my mother popped and gasped at the smoke girl brace'n' 'gainst a stainless grab bar and eye'n' porno-perv at her own reflection.

"Paul Joseph, what are you doing? Are you trying to hurt yourself again? Get back in that bed until the doctors decide it is a good idea for you to be walking around. The last thing we need is for you to fall and gash open your other arm."

I had forgot 'bout the suture. When reflect'n', the changes were so distract'n' that I hadn't recked the bandage around my upper arm, but there it was. It was a wide white bandage wrapped several times 'round my upper arm. It must had been recent replaced 'cause my arm muscles were leaner and the original would have slid down. My mother badgered till I forced myself to stop eye'n' the reflection and negotiated back to the bed. When I settled, my mother plopped the chair 'side the bed.

"Paul Joseph, the doctor has spoken to me. She is coming in soon to explain to you what she thinks is going on and then you are probably going to be discharged. She can't see any reason to keep you hospitalized, but she can explain it better than I can. Now sit up and try to be kind. I just don't know where I went wrong with you, but at least be kind when the doctor comes in. I saw Father Antonio in the hall and he said you were obstinate and unrepentant. My own son, disrespectful to a priest—a priest who is only trying to help you— a priest who cares so much for us. What has become of you?"

"He prayed me like an animal. I ain't no animal."

"Your father died and that was a blow to all of us. Father Antonio says that grief takes many forms. But drug use? This is completely unacceptable."

'fore my mother could continue chastise'n', 'cuse'n', and 'mind'n' me that I were grieve'n', the doctor entered. She donned a white coat and had a stethoscope. She weren't smoke like the ER doc, but she were serious as a tsunami and eyed like she hadn't cracked a joke in twenty.

"Paul Joseph, I'm Doctor Phillips. I've been the one who's been looking into what's going on with you since you were transferred up here from the ER. So, let's start with a few questions I need to ask you. Do you think you can answer some questions for me?"

I nodded. My mother posted right there to assure compliance and respect. Doctor Phillips posted at the foot and I hid my girl tits by hoist'n' the quilt to my shoulders.

"Paul Joseph, we need to know what you took and how long you have been using?"

"Why does everyone think I'm on drugs? I ain't use'n'. I ain't on nothing."

My mother buried her head in her hands.

"See what my son has become, doctor? A self-destructive liar. May God have mercy on him."

Doctor Phillips walked over and patted my mother on the back.

"Do you see what you are doing to those who love you? We really need to know what you are taking."

I spilled in as calm and steady of a voice as I could muster.

"Doctor, I'm honestly not take'n' no drugs. You can test me. You want pee in a cup? I don't know how to convince everyone that I ain't."

Thankfully, Doctor Phillips didn't want pee in a cup 'cause after I offered that volunteer, I 'membered 'bout the shrunken area and reddened with some embarrassment.

"We have tested you, Paul Joseph. You have more estrogen in your blood than three women combined. You also have a remarkable decrease in testosterone. This accounts for your physical changes even though it is hard to explain why they have happened so fast and why the rapid hair growth."

Mother eyed up.

"The Lord works in mysterious ways. It is not for us to understand everything. We must trust in the Lord."

"Well, that may be the only explanation here, but medically, my guess is that Paul Joseph has been using drugs that some dealer decided to lace with estrogen. Why? I have no idea. Maybe he thought it would be funny. Maybe he just wanted to make his supply last longer by cutting it and for some reason he got a hold of a bunch of estrogen. But laced drugs, we see all the time. It's not like your average drug dealer is the most ethical person walking around. The weird thing is we can't figure out what drug Paul Joseph was taking. There are no traces of the drugs we test for in his system. No meth, no cannabis, no cocaine, no hallucinogens, nothing like that. What scares me is this indicates there's either a new drug out there that we don't know about, or that the estrogen is in some way masking the drug and causing a negative test result. In either case, this is a huge red flag. If the dealers are figuring out a way for people to use and not be detected by testing, the implications are major. Think performance enhancing drugs alone. How would we ever know which athletes are clean? If it's a new drug, we might just not be sure what we're looking for so maybe we are looking right at it, but can't see it. And if it's new, we have no idea of its temporary and potential lasting impact on the user."

Doctor Phillips eyed at me.

"We need to know what it is, Paul Joseph. This is serious stuff."

"Doctor, I honest ain't on no drugs."

My mother 'gain buried her face in her hands and wept.

"Paul Joseph, why are you being like this?"

Doctor Phillips continued to stroke my mother's back and console.

"I'm so sorry that your son is acting this way, but under the circumstances, all I can do is recommend counseling and send him home. There's really nothing wrong with him that we can treat here in the hospital, and until he comes clean..."

Doctor Phillips eyed at me and repeated.

"Until he comes clean, he's just going to have to deal with the estrogen and how it is impacting his body."

Say'n' there ain't nothing wrong, discharge'n' me, counsel'n'— it were all Tiny Tim crazy talk and I knowed it.

"Doctor, believe me, you got to, I ain't on no drugs. What 'bout my arm? Gashed it open and didn't even know. What 'bout that?"

"I've thought about that, Paul Joseph, I have thought about that, and my best educated guess is that whatever you are taking is either partially designed to numb your body, or has the side effect of body numbness. I'd say that your un-awareness of the injury raises additional concerns about the dangers of this drug you are taking."

"I ain't."

Doctor Phillips continued to pontificate her theory concern'n' what were happen'n'. My mother reduced to a quiet sob'n' mess.

"Look Paul Joseph, estrogen doesn't just suddenly appear in the bodies of adolescent boys. It got there somehow. So the numbness could also be from something the drug was laced with, or from the drug itself. But you have already decided that you are not going to talk to me, or your mother."

"Or Father Antonio."

My mother chimed.

"Yes, or your priest. There is nothing I can do. I understand your father died not too long ago. Maybe you are grieving. Talking to a counselor could really help you understand what you are going through."

She turned her attention to my mother.

"I'm going to write up the discharge orders and the name of a good counseling service I'm familiar with. I recommend Paul Joseph see someone and the sooner the better. It might also be prudent to keep him home for a while. Assuming he doesn't stash his supply in your home, you might at least disrupt his ability to purchase and use his drugs. Good luck Mrs. Rizzo."

'fore she exited, Doctor Phillips leaned in, put her yap near my ear and spilled low 'nough that my mother couldn't 'ear.

"Doing this to your own mother, shame on you Paul Joseph, shame on you."

Then she erected and stepped out. Father Antonio returned with a shopping bag, handed it to my mother and questioned if he should step out while I dressed.

My mother spilled that maybe they both should. She pushed the call button and dropped the bag on the floor.

"Paul Joseph, you'll find everything you need in this bag. Now get dressed. You're being discharged."

Father Antonio slid an arm 'round my mother's waist and aided her out. I struggled to slide from the bed. The grandmother nurse returned.

"Oh dear, let me help you."

She 'proached and aided me to my feet.

"Now let's get you dressed."

'fore I could protest, she dropped the hospital gown off me and I were post'n' there complete nude. Instinctive I cupped my shrunken area but then realized my girl tits were full on. The grandmother nurse were unfazed. She reached into the shopping bag, removed a white pair of girl underpants and a white bra.

"Do you think you can get these on, or do you need help?"

I posted there frozen. She bent down, lifted my leg an inch off the floor and slid my foot thru the leg hole of the panties. After do'n' the same thing with my other leg, she tugged the panties up over my hips. In the panties where a typical bulge would be was barely a noticeable bump.

"Now hold your arms straight out in front of you."

I complied, and she slipped the bra on me, maneuvered back, and hooked it in place.

"Is that comfortable?"

She questioned as she moved back in front of me and adjusted the cups to better support my girl tits.

"This ain't your regular bra, is it, sweetie?"

I muted.

"Well, it'll have to do till you get home at least."

She produced a Sacred Heart girl polo from the bag and aided me pull it over my head. The Sacred Heart plaid skirt were next. It had an adjustable waist and the grandmother nurse set it. Once that were fastened and straightened, she aided me to a chair, bent, slipped little bobby socks on my feet and then slipped my feet into white Keds sneakers and tied them. They was too small but she horned them on and overtightened the laces. She posted up, walked behind and brushed my hair.

"You have such beautiful hair. But all young women have beautiful hair. Appreciate it when you have it. It will eventually thin out and gray, so appreciate it. You really are quite a beautiful young woman. Oh to be young again. You're on the thin side though. You're not one of those girls who starve themselves to look pretty are you? Take it from me, it ain't worth it. No guy is worth giving up a good piece of chocolate cake for."

The nurse rambled and brushed and finished with the hair pulled back in a ponytail.

A skinny orderly with acne scars and smoker's teeth pushed a wheelchair in. He were preceded by my mother and Father Antonio.

"Well young lady, it's your lucky day. I'm going to chauffeur you right out of this hospital and into the sunlight."

The orderly moved the chair beside, and with the nurse's aid, they plopped me in the wheelchair. The orderly managed to brush one of my girl tits as he positioned me. Facts is I suspected it was purposeful but can't prove it. I was grump and grapes and in no mood. I batted at the perv to warn that he'd better cool. The grandmotherly nurse ignored it. My mother and Father Antonio were oblivious eye'n' and hug'n' each other suppose in consol. 'fore the orderly pushed out into the hall, my mother pruded me to vice my legs and sit lady-like. The orderly patted my arm and clicked his tongue like I was purpose-spread for a free show. With my thighs wedged, the orderly rolled me out the hospital. He aided me into the back seat of the Chrysler. His paws were grope and slime.

"Young lady, you're giving quite a show there."

The orderly winked and chuckled as he lewded at my Sacred Heart plaid skirt that had rode up expose'n' my white panties.

"I work here, but hey, a dude's going to look if it's right in front of his face."

I tugged my skirt.

"Screw you, pervert."

The orderly laughed and reached across to fasten the seatbelt. He brushed both my girl tits with his arm. That one was purpose 'cause he didn't have no poker face.

"Don't fuck'n' touch me."

'fore he shut the door, he cupped himself and spewed that he'd be fine to eye me 'gain. I flipped the finger and he licked his lips.

▲▼▲

'fore we go further here let's confront facts 'bout social pin'n' me misogyny 'cause I didn't rock have'n' no girl body. It were like every spin and I's canceled. I even got skunked by a flash protest outside the Beaver CC commons and that led to pics on all platforms and deeper cancel and facts is even to me work'n with you, Therapeutic Kate, who motivated this auto-bio ink that nobody else is supposed to be crack'n' but might be. 'gardless, it seems there weren't nothing I could do right. The trans vitriol and then the fem vitriol. I didn't do nothing to warrant nothing, but it were there. I can't do nothing 'bout it, but it still funks and that's facts. So diverge but necessary diverge 'cause I's got to defend.

▲ ▼ ▲

When we Chryslered home, I were still Heinz 57 at the perv and unsteady as a one-legged G.I. Joe. My mother aided me to my room. I plopped on the bed. My mother spewed that I RQD to chill and then she vacated. Finally I were solitaire. I rolled onto my back and struggled out of the Sacred Heart girl uni and the girl underwear. It took time to claw out of the bra, but I eventually pulled it around enough that I could fumble the hooks. I took no pride in my naked body. Porno-perv'n' myself after that hospital perv sitch were no longer a green. That were a boy-on-boy sitch and even tho the perv didn't even know it, I did and it cracked me deep. If I ever eyed that perv 'gain a fist in the nose would be my greet'n'. So here's more of the nowhere to turn conundrum. I don't rock boys. That's just my natural. It don't mean boys who rock boys is bad. But that group has canceled me too. So it's facts that social is alway toss'n' contra, but I ain't anti nothing 'cept anti me misrepresent'n'. I ain't no transphobe. I ain't no misogyny. I ain't no homophobe. I'm just a dude who's had an irregular sitch un'countable. I'm sorry, but I's into girls from a dude perspect, that means I want to pop with them not be them and that ain't misogyny contra to social and the Beaver CC skunk. That's intentional diverge 'cause it RQs to be creeded 'cause no one ain't 'ear'n' me 'cause they play I'm low cog on 'count of my vernacular. Social memes it. It ain't fly to be the butt. But Therapeutic Kate advises I got to keep ink'n' this out so back to past tense.

▲ ▼ ▲

Sprawled naked on the bed, I were weak and fatigue and shame. I climbed under the comforter and hauled it up to my neck. I eyed my room. 'bove the headboard were the crucifix that had hanged 'bove my sleep'n' head for my whole life. 'hind the horizontal cross beam were a palm from last year's Palm Sunday. It were looped and tied. Every Palm Sunday, 'long with all the other palms behind all the other crucifixes, it is replaced. My mother sacks the year-olds and RQs me to haul them to school to gift to Father Antonio who adds them to the used pile and burns them into the soot that he smears on brows on Ash Wednesdays. It were full circle and 'nother reason soot smeared on foreheads was bunk. I'd spec whose palm ashes we were wear'n'. Were Jessica wear'n' soot from the palms that once hanged over my bed, or my mother's bed, or the bed of the smelly octogenarian who was always two words back at Mass?

'side the crucifix was the Liverpool FC flag that my father bought for me when he bumped Europe. I were five or six when the obsession to vagabond enveloped him. My father had recent kilt on a two mill property and raked it. He banked most but kept a side pile. I possessed his hand-sprawled pack list:

1. solid hiking boots
2. wool socks
3. underwear
4. pants with zippered legs
5. tech shirts
6. toothbrush and TP
7. a bed roll
8. passport
9. cash

My mother 'members that at one supper he proclamated she and me that he were bug'n' the day next to bounce Europe for forty. He labeled it a pilgrimage—claim'n' that if Jesus did the desert for forty, he could do Europe for forty. I were too tyke to comprehend. If I were to eye a float'n' basketball back then it might not even register as magic. That's how tyke I were. I were 'nough to 'member my mother be'n' none too happy, but he were hobo-bum'n' for forty and that were that. I 'member question'n' if he'd present me something and hug'n' 'fore he darted. He returned forty later stained, emaciated and unkempt, but he had 'membered to present me: the Liverpool FC flag. I had just noviced peewee soccer and were already iron, but I knowed nothing 'bout Europe football and had never eyed no pro match. Present tense, I have grown to 'preciate the flag and 'cause of the flag, I's a fan. Odd how something like that can patriot allegiance. My father just as easy could have presented me a Manchester United or a Real Madrid flag and then I probably would be follow'n' that team, but he presented the Liverpool FC flag and present tense that's my allegiance.

I 'member him aid'n' me hang it. He were road weary and fatigue. He didn't chow or unpack. He strolled home, proclamated that he were back, hugged me and my mother, and presented me the flag out the top of his pack.

"Where should we hang this?"

He palmed my hand and led me to the garage where he localed brads and a hammer. We punched brads into plaster and hanged the flag. It were my first time with tools, and I were gimp. I dented the wall when I missed the brad completely. My father were kind and patient and repeated brads whenever I crooked one. I eyed at those four thin little brads that we had tacked 'most ten years past and half flashed. Then I eyed at the other things in my room. My bookcase stuffed with my child books—Harry Potters, a picture set of *The Chronicles of Narnia*, my children's Bible, gift kid-books and a wee collection of Marvel comics—I once popped that I'd collect Marvel comics, but soon waned interest 'cause I jived do'n' 'stead of plop'n'. I certainly weren't no 40 hour reader. The bookcase were more just a storage area of mementos. Facts here is that you don't have to be no book lover to be IQ. Lumps always post the contra, but it's a misdirect. IQ is IQ. Books don't elevate that. My dad were IQ and I inherited, so therefore and that's facts. Diverge to re-spill that social's always paint'n' me out as low cog which ain't facts. If I were low cog I'd not eye no irony in ink'n' all this when I ain't respectful of read'n'. So facts is I'm IQ with some limits is what Therapeutic Kate diagnoses and they's MD IQ so contra that fact.

'side the bookcase were a small wood desk that held my laptop, a desk light, and a few Sacred Heart textbooks. I eyed my closet were ajar since a ratty sneaker were prevent'n' it from close'n' and my dresser drawers were half shut with clean clothes hang'n' out the tops like plants grow'n' out of some tiered pot. Dirty clothes were haphazard wherever I happened to have shed. I were a slob and that's facts I don't like to record but ink the entire Therapeutic Kate has instructed and I's try'n' to follow the plan. Sos it's a fact: I's a slob.

In the corner were my soccer bag. It were unzipped. I could eye the World Cup ball I saved coin for and my scruffy boots. The boots were elite coinage, and it weren't till I hit varsity that my father shelled. He were cancered and on the couch flip'n' daytime TV when I homed. He enquired why I beamed. I told him I hit the cut, and he motioned for me to hug him. The next day, when I homed, the boots were sit'n' on the bed in a wrapped box with a card that reported how proud he were of me.

The sun was set'n' and my room shadowed. My mother had not returned, which were fine, and as dusk began to replace the sun, I 'tempted focus on the room and not on my body.

I drifted and dreamed of pedal bikes and public swims. My mother woke me in the AM. In sleep, the comforter had slipped down and my chest were exposed. My mother plopped on the side of the bed and hit a gentle shake of my shoulder. I realed the sitch, grabbed the comforter and tugged it over my girl tits. My mother had tea bag eyes and thick black-gray hair that needed a brush. She were in a robe and house slippers and I specced she had little sleep. She had brought me a tray of scramble, rye toast, bacon, and hash browns. The hash browns were her scratch on special. A tall glass of OJ spilled a bit when she positioned the tray.

"Paul Joseph, I know you're grieving, and I've been thinking that maybe I have not been a very good mother to you ever since your father got sick. I see now that this is all your way of telling me to see you and give you the comfort you deserve. From now on, Paul Joseph, I'm going to be the mother you need."

She hugged me and pontificated that she loved me and kissed my forehead. I didn't know where the soot went but it must've been wiped off in the semi-private 'cause neither her nor me had it no more. She instructed me to eat and dress. She spilled Father Antonio had excused me from school, but that it were a Friday of Lent and she would like us to hit the noontime Stations of The Cross.

She bugged. I sat up and 'tempted to scarf breakfast, but after a few bites of scramble, I nauseated. I had disappointed my mother over the top and she were guilt that this transform was somehow on her. She typically were not no doter or an especially affectionate mother, but it were crystal that she were implement'n' a novel strat. I give her cred for that even tho it didn't last too long. Queasy, I forced myself to scarf most of the vittles and to gulp half the OJ so as not to disappoint. When I tried to post to dress, I clumsily knocked the tray and clattered the dishes and the juice smash'n' it all 'gainst the floor. It were noise enough to 'lert. My mother quick arrived and eyed the shard dishes and the remains splat 'side the bed. I figured she'd blow. My mother had small patience for spills and messes and prided a spotless and orderly abode. Alternative to blow'n', she creeded that 'cidents happen and she went to fetch supplies.

Like a hired maid, she red up the mess. She repeated that it were no problem and that things happen. When she were finished, she employed me to dress so we could hit the Stations. I questioned her what I should wear. She rummaged my drawers and found soccer warm-ups and a hoodie.

"You'll probably be a bit warm in this get up, but it's loose enough to hide your changes, and you can tuck your hair into the back of the hoodie."

"You OK for me to wear my own clothes?"

"Dear, you should be comfortable. I know I shouldn't say this, but I think I was wrong to listen to Father Antonio at the hospital. The outfit was his idea. He said that if you wanted to be a girl that you should have to dress like one. He thought the embarrassment would get you to confess about the drugs. With your father gone, I just sort of let him make the call."

She teared up a bit and even tho she had masterfully red the mess I'd made of the breakfast, she presented helpless and without a rudder. I spec that may have been the first instance I cogitated 'bout how my father kick'n' impacted her. Up to then, I stayed in my point-of-view. I had fret 'bout who'd taxi me to soccer and how soon I could hang with my group. My father were always cancer on the couch. My system was hooked to the TV he were always flip'n' and game'n' were my vegetable. I resented all the 'tention my mother had to give him, and I resented scarf'n' leftovers and cafeteria vittles. When my father were admitted to the hospital 'cause the pain were severe and I had to cut Jimmy V's bonfire, I were none too smiles and plopped in his semi-private with my arms cross Heinz 57 'nough to eye-kill a cockroach. The entire were nails on her too and maybe it were time for me to mature and realize that my father kick'n' weren't solo 'bout me. I eyed at my mother. Tears seeped out 'hind her dark browns.

"Ma, I'm really regretful 'bout everything. I know you miss him too."

My mother folded into the comment and embraced me tight. She hugged me for some time. I were just in my under-shorts, but I folded and briefly out-of-minded the long hair, shrunken area, and girl tits.

My mother released, dabbed eyes with fingers and instructed me to dress or we'd be truant for Stations. She fingered my hair and pecked my forehead 'fore lug'n' out supplies and garbage. I shut the door. I were dizzy and numb as if I had recently tumbled off the tilt-a-whirl at a street fair, and, after struggle'n', I emerged out of the room don in athletic gear resemble'n' like the dude I thought I were—long as no one eyed close. My mother were in the kitchen load'n' the dishwasher. She had touched-up makeup, brushed hair and were wearing clean slacks and a blouse. She eyed stable and adult.

I 'preciated the change, and I 'preciated insight into the Sacred Heart girl uni. It were Father Antonio who put her to that shenanigan as my father would have labeled it. 'fore we hit and while still sympathy, I eyed at my mother.

"Ma, I really don't know what's happen'n', but it ain't nothing I've done intentionally to get revenge at you. You have to believe me. I wouldn't never do something like that to you."

"Death is hard, Paul Joseph. If we can't rely on our families, who can we rely on?"

My mother questioned if I wanted to drive. I admitted that I didn't judge I were reliable. I's walked to the passenger door, opened it and promptly slammed it latched on my fingers. The door rebounded as my fingers rejected the 'tempt latch. I reached, grabbed and shut the door correct 'fore it 'curred that I had just smashed my fingers in a car door. I didn't sense ache as I examined. Four fingers were badly bruised and swell'n' like bubbles. I were like a tyke eye'n' a 'toon. I eyed the mangled hand which disassociated as mine and which didn't feel. My mother eyed what went down and popped her door, walked in the house, and 'turned with ice.

"You'd better put ice on that to help the swelling."

I palmed the ice and pressed on the swell but like the damage itself, the ice didn't feel neither.

"You must be in so much pain, Paul Joseph. But let me be here for you. Hurting yourself won't make the pain go away."

"Ma, I ain't done this on purpose. You have to believe me. I don't know what's happen'n'."

"When we are grieving, we sometimes do things on purpose that we don't realize we are doing on purpose. You are obviously struggling, Paul Joseph. I just didn't realize how bad off you are. Do you think you can still attend the Stations of the Cross or do you need to stay here?"

The Stations of the Cross is strange and depressing plus kneel'n', genuflect'n', and rise'n' were like soccer condition'n', yet my mother were 'tempt'n' kind and I knowed she desired me to 'company so I reported that I judged I could stay the course. She hopped the Chrysler and motored us to church. Father Antonio did the service which were attended by a handful of devouts. Mother permitted me to sit thru all the rise and kneel once she eyed me struggle'n'.

After, my mother and me plopped a pew till Father Antonio 'proached for an update. My mother theorized that with God's aid we'd be aces and Father Antonio nodded, palmed my mother's hand and patted. He eyed at me as if 'tempt'n' to eye if I'd morphed back. I crossed arms in front of my girl tits and lowered head to keep him guess'n' and uncertain.

He palmed my shoulder.

"Paul Joseph, remember, the Lord helps those who help themselves."

I resisted the urge to shake him off. Now that I knowed how he were likely to advise my mother concern'n' my sitch, I desired to remain far away as I could. I knowed there would be interactions like this, but I weren't go'n' to prolong 'em by spill'n' nothing. A threatened opossum play'n' dead were my strat. I were stoic and waited for Father Antonio to unpalm my shoulder and depart. Eventually, he offered a blessed day and turned to duties.

When we Chryslered home, I went to my room and other than to emerge to attend Sunday Mass with my mother, I 'mained bed till the follow Friday when my mother 'tended the Stations of the Cross solo. She had kinded, nurtured and gentled all seven, but I sensed that she were slow surrender'n' her strat 'cause nothing were change'n' with me. Aside the arm gash heal'n' and gradual regain'n' smashed finger usage, I weren't display'n' no signs of lose'n' long hair nor the girl tits, not to mention regrowth down there which like I said is the entire and since I'm spill'n' the entire, bad and good, the facts got to be facts.

Contra to morph'n' return, I felt turned-up in the shape my body were assume'n'. My hips widened and my broad shoulders narrowed and softened. I had rubbed with Jessica enough to know that athletic girls was firm and muscle cores, but that there were little they could affect to rip triceps and biceps. Like Jessica's, my arms were thin and narrow, more prairie than hill. I also knowed Jessica's skin, when we rubbed, were soft and silk. My skin were sandpaper comparison, but eyes shut, my new skin were Jessica's. Face and chest hair shed off. No needed to razor and the more I touched myself the more I were Jessica satin. Like previous, I 'mained quite shrunken down below, but fortunately my mother neither hadn't imagined check'n' or were over embarrass to enquire.

For an entire seven my mother continued food in bed, fresh sheets daily and she once meticulously red my room, under my supervision 'course. She assented to my preferences of what went where. Sometimes she would plop on the side of the bed and palm her cool hand on my forehead and 'ssure me that she loved me and that she were there for me. Yet, most times I were solo with thoughts which were depress, confusion, shame, and lonely.

▲▼▲

I know this upcome'n' fact will be jag to swallow. It might even be jaggier than the transform facts. But nobody can cred my long hair and girl tits and the shrunken down under and then turn and protest that I ain't capable of comprehension—that I ain't IQ? But here's facts for contra. Future tense at Beaver CC, in the same class that cracked *The Metamorphosis*, I were RQD to crack *Frankenstein*. I 'member first be'n' surprised that the book cover didn't have no knob monster representation. It didn't have no green skin electrode-jut-from-neck freak. There weren't no scars or chunky clods. 'stead, this creature were grace and athletic. It had long flow hair and bulge muscles which tensed and flared as he were scale'n' rock. This weren't the cinema Frankenstein that I knowed. While I were peruse'n', alienate feel'n's and isolate feel'n's refloated. I were mirror of the creature, plus I too had felt I were absolute solo, that no one else were like me or could possible the groove I were groove'n'. We all lug crosses, but who among has woke one AM the opposite. Mothers and fathers kick it constant, and buckets of kids gets affect from their parents' kick. A parent kick when I were adolescent were a sucker punch low, but it were also no sucker punch low that others ain't absorbed. Some absorb it private and end down for the count. Some get up and fight 'nother round. Most have corner aid for water and strat and courage. Who were in my corner? Who were aid'n' me to absorb this second blow? Certainly not Father Antonio and course not my own father who were six months kicked and show'n' no signs of resurrection. My mother were 'tempt'n', but there were something I RQD that weren't on her menu. The creature RQD a companion and as much as the wack 'tempted to satisfy, it weren't on his menu neither. While crack'n' that book, I realized that even if I had knowed what to order, my mother couldn't 've cooked it. This were outside her. What I RQD, she could not supply. That ten days in my bedroom under her ministry were comfort, but it were also a mere rest stop. It weren't no apex. I were stagnant. My father threw hate at sloth, and I then were animated sloth. I could not prone the rest of the ride. I would RQ action. I cogitated bunches. But what could I do? Should I skedaddle and attempt to exist like a girl, never spill'n' to anyone 'bout my past tense? Would I eventual wake up one AM to find that whatever had come over me were exit, and I were boy returned? If I skedaddled and that happened would I RQ to skedaddle 'gain? How'd I get vittles and where would I reside? And Jessica? I fawned Jessica like teens fawn. We were ideal and optimism and creeded fairytale happily-ever-afters. We'd be always fawn. We'd never bick 'bout bank or employ or inanes. We'd be exalt. Would I soccer 'gain? If I did, what team would I be on? The girls? The boys? How could I get to college? You don't know what happened to Jessica 'cause I ain't spilled the end there, but you do know I landed at Beaver CC, well at least till the skunk. But that's diverge. I momentarily cogitated maybe I could 'tend back to school like everything were reg, but I knowed I weren't gonna pull that charade. 'side be'n' singled for post'n' goals or kill'n' on the pitch, I ducked the lime, and I cert were not a martyr. Facts is I were a chip when I were Heinz 57, but when I were ice, I'd merely join and follow. Even when I weren't ice and I was all Heinz 57'n' it up in some noodle's face, it were 'bout that particular sitch. I ain't the type to fret 'bout causes. I's ink'n' this, and that's facts, but I ain't ink'n' it to insight and aid no one but myself. I's ink'n' 'cause Therapeutic Kate thinks it'll help. Nothing more.

Therapeutic Kate asked me about heroes once and I 'member spill'n' to them 'bout MLK and RBG and shakers similar. We had history class on them. These people were impress and courage. If Nelson Mandela popped girl tits and long hair not to mention had a shrunken area down, he'd still contra apartheid. If Malcolm X popped a massive 'fro, a plaid pantsuit and yellow stilettos, he'd remain, "It's liberty or death. It's freedom for everybody or freedom for nobody," and if anyone had the guts to question 'bout the girl tits, he'd redirect them to spot on the cause, that girl tits or no girl tits, the issue were racism, and, "If you're not ready to die for it, put the word 'freedom' out of your vocabulary." But I weren't no Malcolm X, nor Ginsburg, nor King, nor Mandela. If I were sent up for twenty-seven, I'd protect myself certain but when I freedomed out I'd be worse for wear, not prepared to 'ssume the role of South Africa king. Nope, those weren't no typicals. They was born with fortitude—I were born with attitude but not fortitude. There's a difference and that's the facts that I learnt from Therapeutic Kate. I were a boy with a kicked father who had mysteriously morphed into a girl and were go'n' to fight out of that sitch, but if Jimmy V were morphed into a girl, I'd just be pissed that we lost our center back. I wouldn't be lead'n' no sit-in fight for boy/girl rights.

I cogitated further and recalled Marie Curie and Therapeutic Kate instructed to explore those edges 'cause here were a girl who got given two Nobels. She's not merely the only two time girl, but the only two time period. She 'scaped out of Poland to educate in Paris where she were eyed as a 'spicious foreigner and hated on 'cause of be'n' girl. She even illed from exposure to radiation. But she eventually made anti-cancer procedures. Father Dominic pontificated us that during WWI, Marie Curie installed x-rays in ambulances and motored them to the front. I 'member 'bout that. She were courage. My father were 'bout to final kick for good when Father Dominic pontificated all that 'bout Marie Curie and it resonated 'cause of the cancer that remained me in a straight jacket. A sloth looker-on. Marie Curie were active, and I were passive and that were shame.

In my room, cogitate'n' 'bout Marie Curie were when I re-shamed. What did I have to pity 'bout? Shouldn't I tackle it and hustle on? *Suck it up and get on with it* were my father's motto whenever the sitch hit rocky, and I cogitated I were the type to embrace that motto, but like the cancer, this body morph were not a rocky patch I'd just suck up and overcome, and those facts were shame. Where were courage and bravery and Saint Peter? I surmise that most teen lumps creed we are courage and noble and martyr material, and maybe

that's why we flock military when there's war. We is passion-
ate and concretely creed values and that sacrifice is noble.
It's a frown day when we pop and eye our cowardness. I realized that in my bedroom as I passed those isolate days, yet it
were later that Therapeutic Kate helped me fully comprehend how most lumps twin Victor and why we entirely de-
spise the creature.

▲▼▲

My isolation and pity stretched and by Thurs AM of the
second seven, I could eye my mother, who were still 'tempt-
t'n' nurture, were soon to tire of my slack. I deferred school
and had only really been out of bed to shower and hit Sunday Mass which I would have truanted if I hadn't wanted to
try and do a kind for my mother. I suppose she cogitated
that if she overwhelmed me with nurture and stayed patient
that I'd return dude, but that were miscalculation. Contra,
my girl tits growed slight firmer, my hair growed thicker and
I were still shrunken down below.

▲▼▲

I didn't know nothing 'bout long hair and my mother
wershed it for me. She then brushed it and braided it into a
solo thick that lay down my back like a python. With my
braid and my hood, my past tense face, minus the peach fuzz
were recognizable, and I eyed at it in reflect and 'gain wondered what were happen'n'.

It were a Tuesday late AM, of seven three when my mother knocked and entered with Father Antonio. I were dressed
but still under covers. I were text'n' Jessica who was in study
at Sacred Heart. I fibbed I had the flu and would probs be
truant at least for the rest of the seven. I had also texted my
soccer coach and Jimmy V with the same scoop. I knowed it
were false facts and here's more support of my ink'n' true
facts present tense 'cause those false facts is be'n' admitted

now and if I's admitt'n' false facts present tense then that's contra hurled at lumps who assert that this entire therapeutic auto-bio is false facts, and if no lumps is crack'n' this, then this is for you, Therapeutic Kate, sos you know that I's toe'n' the line you chalked.

▲ ▼ ▲

When my mother and Father Antonio entered, I eyed up confusion from the phone. Father Antonio stayed post and my mother plopped the desk chair.

"Paul Joseph, this isn't working."

"What ain't work'n'?"

"You're not getting better and allowing you to hide out here in your bedroom is not healthy. At first I thought maybe you just needed some time to sort things out, that maybe with nurturance and rest you'd start to open up and talk with me about what's going on, but that's not happening."

"Son, do you have drugs in your room?"

Father Antonio cut as serious as a supreme court judge.

"What?"

"Your mother has cleaned every inch of this room, and she hasn't found anything, but obviously you're still using. So how are you getting the drugs?"

Father Antonio eyed down at me. I eyed direct and felt the Heinz 57 brew'n'.

"There ain't no drugs. I told that already."

My mother clammed my palm and were really try'n' support and compassion, but her patience were clearly thin ice.

"Paul Joseph, then what about the changes to your body? How can you explain that? You are not changing back so what else are we to assume?"

My mother lowered head and 'peared defeated like a used sophomore the day after the prom. Father Antonio 'proached and palmed her shoulder.

"Is someone sneaking in at night and supplying you?"

I shook my head stubbornly and defiantly like a dog that ain't ashamed 'bout the turd on the rug. My mother eyed at the floor.

"Grief is hard, but drugs are not the answer, Paul Joseph. Look what they have done to you. Do you want this body? Do you like being away from your friends and off the soccer team?"

I squeezed my mother's grip. I dropped a frustration tear.

"'course I don't want it like this. I don't know what's happen'n', but there ain't no drugs. Why won't you believe me?"

With my free hand I wipered tears from my face. I were full Heinz 57 which typically didn't include no bawl'n' but this were overwhelm'n'. I weren't sure if I were bawl'n' frustration toward my mother and Father Antonio's contra, or at my inability to comprehend what were pop'n'. Either barricaded a plausible alt-drug explanation, and my mother and Father Antonio, be'n' Catholic and all, creeded that plausible explanations were expected.

Still eye'n' at the floor, my mother squeezed my hand.

"We thought this might be your reaction. Father Antonio and I have discussed this at length, and we have decided that our best approach is, if you insist on being a girl..."

My mother paused and tried to steady her voice.

"...is to treat you like a girl."

I bolted straight and my bawl'n' stopped. I were full on Heinz 57.

"What you mean?"

"Father Antonio has spoken with the headmaster at Our Lady of Perpetual Sorrows and has arranged for you to transfer there starting Monday."

"Ma, that's an all girls school."

"Yes it is, but you obviously can't go back to Sacred Heart. What would people think? No, we think it is better that you have a fresh start at a place where no one will know that you have not always been a girl. We are telling you now so you have some time to adjust."

"Ma, that's wack. I ain't go'n' to no Perpetual Sorrows. What are you pull'n'? What 'bout my group? What 'bout Jessica? What 'bout soccer?"

Father Antonio was catch'n' none of what I were throw'n'. He pointed his fat Liberace ring finger. The large emerald ring eyed absurd like jewelry on a corpse or a silky pink carnation fixed to the handle of an ax.

"Son, this is your choice. If you want to stay at Sacred Heart, you know what to do. Otherwise, it's time to move on with your life. You can't stay in bed forever. We must face our problems, not hide from them."

I 'sidered rip'n' Father Antonio locales he could insert his Liberace ring but my mother were there and I curtailed my Heinz 57 since it weren't aid to punch. Slur would just make them remain and I RQD isolation to strat. They pontificated for a few 'bout how this were facts my decision and 'bout how much of a hurdle grief can be, but once they seen I weren't interested in their religion, they tasked me to cogitate it. Father Antonio aided my mother from the chair and, with his arm wrapped, ushered her. I rolled on my side, faced the wall and lid my eyes. I knowed Father Antonio had put my mother to this. My father never would have ceded that this were a plausible option, but he weren't 'round to strat with my mother and so she were now bet'n' on Father Antonio to aid her decide. At that present tense, I recollect resentment 'bout my father kick'n' and leave'n' me fly'n' solo. I knowed he could not just choose not to kick, and that that were irrational, but it stoked me that 'cause he kicked I were now be'n' parented by Father Antonio 'stead of a fact father. How could he kick and do this to me? He had to know that things would pop after he were kicked, that sitchs would 'rise in which I RQD aid, but he kicked anyway and that were 'nother Heinz 57 moment. I cogitated all into afternoon 'bout how my father had abandoned and 'bout how I really RQD him then. As I lay there throw'n' hate at my father for kick'n', the memory of opt'n' out Hord from the litter at the breeder crashed my mind. I were a little tyke, maybe five or six, and my father and mother Chryslered me rural. They inkled me a surprise. I were pop'n' like corn as we motored in front of a paintless farmhouse. A wack in suspenders, a rat straw hat and a string gray beard shook my father's palm. He walked us to an unpainted outbuilding where there were a tricolor Beagle and five pups in chicken wire jail. They were on straw and the bitch were nurse'n'. My mother eyed at me and questioned which one I opted. I were first confused and said I opted the big one. The old wack in the ratty straw hat gurgled and then my mother facted me that the big one were not salable 'cause that were the bitch, and she RQD to remain to grow pups for other tykes. Once I certained that, I eyed close at each pup and eventually indexed a white and chocolate runt that seemed to be more sad than the sibs and thus in aid of rescue. The wack scooped him and armed him to me. I cradled the pup to my face, and he slurped my chin. I flashed. My father worked out the sale and in the Chrysler the initial excitement wore off, I 'came sad and bawl'n'. My mother poked why I were bawl'n' and I blabbed to her that I didn't want the dog no more. When she questioned why, I guilted her that the dog belonged with its mother. My father gurgled and 'tempted to pontificate 'bout dogs not be'n' like that, that dogs don't connect to their parents like people. I poked all types of asks 'bout why that were and no matter how much my mother and father 'tempted to make me light, it just didn't make no sense. The other thing that didn't make no jive was where the pup's father were. Redux, my mother and father pontificated 'bout breed'n' procedure, but I were too tyke. Finally, the only 'pease and connect were my father learn'n' me that I subbed the pup's father, that we all RQD fathers and that since the pup didn't have no father, I'd have to fill that bucket. For some reason that clicked me, and I subbed protector, nurturer, and teacher. It took me a while to cogitate up the name Hord, but one day it popped and from that day until we had to kick him down because of kidney fail, he were Hord and I were his father.

I lost Hord 'bout simultaneous to when my father pancreatic-cancered. When him and my mother plopped me down to spill, it were a cold winter day and school were shut due to ice. The announcement of the school shut came in the previous evening, so I late gamed and crashed till lunch. When I climbed up and eyed out the window to gawk at fresh fall snow, I were instead hit with a yard of slush puddles. It were like eye'n' a landscape of puny gray lakes and ice ponds. A heavy thick rain pelted the window. There were wind and a rusted plow waved gray muck high into the air. Its grimy curved blade 'tempted to flip the mess from street to yard. Everything were dismal and dreary, and even tho I 'tempted to visualize green grass and sunshine, as I eyed out that February noon, it were like the sun would never bright 'gain, like ugly would be the new real. My mother bawled as my father, a stoic face, facted that typically pancreatic cancer hit rapid and that he were likely to kick in three to five. He pontificated 'bout voluntary treatment, but that we had to be real and the facts were that recover'n' were bet'n' the dark horse. This dreary ice weather and the news were obvious contra to snow-shut expects. On the eve, I figured a wake up to pure snow and maybe sled with my group or snowball fight or at least trod thru in boots and a parka. Not only were outside a no go by the weather, I were stuck inside with a bawl'n' mother and a father who were 'parently 'bout to cancer out.

I prodded all the prods a thirteen year old might like what the treatments would be, would he have to stop house sell'n', would he still be able to eye me soccer, did he have to hit a wack diet, but in general, it didn't seem real. My father eyed fine and so even tho he reported ill, it were breeze to ignore and eye the physical of my father which looked spec on. Of course, eventually his rock did crumble and he dropped weight and barely ate anything. He jaundiced and 'came listless. He even vomited regular. My mother bought a stack of kidney basins and were sure that one were always within reach of where my father were propped. As he frailed and yellowed, as his thick black hair thinned and eventually fell out completely, I gradually lost the ability to eye this sick weak cancer as my father. He had become a cancer stranger live'n' on the couch, and I were able to distract in my group, soccer and Jessica, and it were like my father dropped on a trip or were busy work'n'. The sick wack at home were just a charity my mother had taken on. Maybe I were just too kid to really understand farewell—to face the decay of the man who up to that point were nurture and protect, but I dealt with it by 'tend'n' it weren't, and I suppose that worked and life progressed relatively normal as he frailed and ashened. Even when he kicked it final and we grounded him, to me the dead lump on the sofa were not my father and the dirt on the coffin were detached. Of course I knowed the facts, but it didn't feel like it were facts. It felt more like at any moment, my father would strut in the house like he had when he 'turned from Europe and presented me, and then go back to regular father. This most lifted me till the transform and then this—the moment I realized that I were be'n' parented by my mother and Father Antonio and be'n' coerced to flip schools and 'tend a girl school. No longer could I pretend my father would materialize from a trip and bail me. No, I were solo, and I had to cogitate what I were go'n' to rock.

There were no way I was go'n' to jive Our Lady of Perpetual Sorrows. I weren't a girl, and I weren't go'n' to live like one. It seemed that if I stayed cloistered that that were exactly what Father Antonio and my mother had strated for me. After an unrest and jumble sixty, I shut and hit slumber to avoid.

I woke to a bright Wednesday AM feel'n' strangely refreshed and energetic. My arm were near healed and my fingers normal. During the night, something switched in my nog and I solved what I RQD. It might not restore dude, but I knowed I needed to skedaddle, to flight, to cogitate solo in isolation. My mother and Father Antonio were not go'n' to solve this puzzle and as long as I stayed in my safe sloth, it weren't go'n' to get no better. And now we's finally back to the cabin that started all this. That's were I plotted flight. It were remote and 'peared a rock seclusion for the short. All I RQD were to pack supplies and map the route. Pack'n' supplies would be slide. I had a soccer duffle which were plenty to gather clothes and vittles. How to get to the cabin were the hurdle. I could take the Chrysler. It were parked for sale, but if I heisted it, I were 'fraid that the heat might hit if my mother telephoned the dis'pearance of me and the Chrysler. I opted 'stead to jack my father's scooter. It were tarped in the garage rear. My father hadn't started it since he cancered and I weren't cert it were in run condition, but I strated that the next time my mother were at Mass or the grocery, I would bust the garage and eval the scooter.

Like the cabin, the scooter were a project. My father had slipped it from a garage of an estate he were break'n'. The owner had kicked it a few years previous. The two adult kids plopped out of town after they swooped and dashed with what they desired. They charged my father to salable the remains. He cashed the scooter, hauled it home, and made me flashlight and fetch philips and sockets, while he wrenched. He stripped it and restored it metallic red after sand'n' to bare metal and prime'n'. He rebuilt the motor, learnt me to snake cables, overhaul the clutch and pry on the tires. When it were finished, the scooter eyed new. With no shell, my father ripped the thing down and up the residential and then let me fling circles in the yard. I dropped it a few 'tempt'n' to navigate the tights, but since it were just turf, I didn't cause nothing serious. Just ruts and they is most healed.

It spun that the thrill were in the resto and not in the toot'n' 'round town, and after bust'n' it 'round for a few sevens, the scooter 'came more a thing stowed and less an amusement or a Chrysler substitute. Then when my father cancered, the scooter, already an old toy, transformed to dead storage tarped behind gypsum four by eights, a wood ladder and busted yard tools. It would RQ time just to surface and then additional to build it back to run order. 'gardless, it seemed like the best option. If I could surface it and spark it, the thing could likely haul me to the cabin and maybe my mother would not even suspect it were heisted which might throw off the bloodhounds.

It were a Friday and still Lent and my mother headed out on her date with Father Antonio at Stations of the Cross. Now that's more facts that I should've been dive'n' into, but it were a side dish and I were eye on the prize and not cogitate'n' the perverse 'specially when it concerned my mother. I gagged future tense when I eyed it straight, but past tense it were a dark closet I weren't crack'n'. I had at least two sixties to surface the scooter and evaluate the condition. With my girl tits and long hair and shrunken area, surface'n' the scooter proved more than I 'ticipated, but after some considerable effort, I had the scooter propped on the center stand and ready for inspection. Of course everything still gleamed new, but the tires were flat and the fuel had probably expired. I fired the compressor and as I waited for pressure, I fiddled the fuel line disconnect. It actually popped slide and expired fuel streamed on my hands and over the little motor 'fore I could pop the hose back. I found a Maxwell House can and managed to drain the remains into it. The tires pressured and held. I sloshed fresh fuel from the mower can and dropped some 40:1. My father had a measurer baggied under the seat and had learnt me the mix during the resto. The only thing remaining were to fire the thing. I choked full and jumped down on the kick five or six times 'fore the motor hit. Black plumes exhausted and I gradual depressed the choke and idled the motor. All this had spanned sixty or more and I slight fretted that my mother might land sooner than expected. I kilt the motor and popped the bedroom feel'n' solid that my escape vehicle were prepped. My mother never garaged, so I didn't bother to underground the scooter. I were mental pack'n' and strat'n' as I soaped the fuel off adequately, but I were slight paranoid my mother would odor the gasoline. I palmed my father's aftershave and splashed my face and hands. It odored musk and vague reminiscent of the only buck I had ever downed. My father were along and we were early sit'n' a tree stand. My father hit black coffee from a stainless mug, and I bit pebbles to stop my teeth chatter. It were autumn cold. We had patienced in that stand numerous to no avail, and I were relative certain that this time also would end after a few sixties of me eye'n' squirrels and birds and rabbit hops, but into my eye popped an eight point. Three does herded by it. My father gently tipped my shoulder and whispered to hit the buck. I merely had a one shot twenty-two, but my father had the .30-30 Winchester. He armed it to me. I had ripped it at beer cans and knowed how to aim. The buck were side face'n'. I gripped the .30-30 and carefully aimed considerable above the back of the foreleg to 'count for the drop. My father had learnt me the heart locale and I knowed it were the likely hit to clean kill. I exhaled slow and gently squeezed the trigger. Even tho I had ripped rifles with my father numerous and I were earplugged, I were startled by the repercuss and the discharge echo. The sixty of absolute peace were suddenly shat. The does hoofed. The buck sprang, hit a few yards, toppled and kicked it. It were a perfect heart-kill. My father prouded me and post times referenced me as the little sniper. We dressed the buck and eventually dredged it to our rental and strung it. I 'membered the musk carcass odor when I slapped the aftershave.

When my mother hit, she came to my room and facted me that I were go'n' to grub supper at table, no longer would she deliver vittles to my room like a servant to a prince. She further facted that I were open'n' school Monday and I RQD to pass the weekend adjust'n' to the open closet and strap'n' 'propriate clothes. She toted clothes and plopped them on the bed.

"I gathered some clothes for you from the church donation center. They aren't the best, but they will do for now. Father Antonio has arranged for us to go to Our Lady of Perpetual Sorrows tomorrow. The headmaster has agreed to meet with us special on a Saturday, show you around, get you scheduled and to set you up with some uniforms. Also,

you need to know that he has only agreed to enroll you under the condition that you stay under the radar and that you
stay off their soccer team. He doesn't want trouble or scandal."

"Ma, I ain't go'n' there. It's a girls school."

"Paul Joseph, you leave me no choice. As long as you continue whatever it is that you are doing, there are going to be
natural consequences."

'fore she shut the door and ordered me to dress for supper, she spilled me that douse'n' my father's aftershave
wouldn't convince no one I were a dude. 'stead of a cheap
trick, I ought to hit the real.

▲▼▲

I shifted the clothes and eyed a mess of girl skirts and
blouses, two bras and an unopened pack of girl underwear.
That were too much, I knowed I had to fly that PM. My
mother, divine inspired by Father Antonio, were heart-at-
tack 'bout this new strat and not only was I not go'n' to don
no more girl clothes, there were no way I were go'n' to be
dragged to the headmaster at Our Lady of Perpetual Sorrows
and enroll in an all girl. I dumped my soccer equipment out
of the duffle and quickly packed all but one of my athletic
pants, some jerseys and tees, socks, underwear and sneakers. I tossed the duffle in the closet, slid into the remaining
pair of athletic pants and Liverpool FC jersey and popped
supper.

My mother scanned the fit.

"Paul Joseph, you are going to need to start dressing ap-
propriately."

"Ma, I ain't wear'n' no girl clothes."

My mother smashed her lips 'gether and widened her
dimples as she swallowed the impulse to sass. It were crystal
she stuck this new phase were a clean open and even tho she
were not happy that I were not wear'n' the girl clothes, she
figured that least supper at the table were a start.

She had fried some chicken and dished it dropped on rice with canned beans on the side. I 'member that supper good. I weren't sure what would future, but I knowed I were to skedaddle that PM. I cogitated that this may be the final supper sit with my mother. I teared and, like condensation on a water glass, when I napkin dabbed, the tears quickly reformed.

My mother hit a small glass of red—something rare— and as we supped, she lit an ounce amount of red to a juice glass and slid me. When my father were 'live, he'd sometimes grant me to have a small red or quarter beer on holidays. When he did, he'd big production of me hit'n' sips. My mother tolerated it as a boy/man rite. She didn't toast tho. Present, she initiated. She hoisted her glass and motioned me to hoist mine. I complied and 'dditional tears dropped.

"Paul Joseph, Father Antonio reminds me, that our faith tells us to be strong and courageous, to not be afraid or discouraged, that the Lord will be with us through whatever happens."

Even tho her preach were more statement than toast, she clinked glass, and we sipped the red. I had sampled little red at that present, but this red ranked tart and odored like a bandage. I swallowed and then over-washed with cow milk.

Att: Therapeutic Kate: this here part is included as more facts that past tense I weren't hit'n' libation. I ain't even liked it when it were free-offered. But that's more diverge.

▲▼▲

"This adjustment is going to be hard for everyone, Paul Joseph, but this too will pass and we can get through it. I know it might seem like I'm pushing you, but you need to trust me and believe me when I tell you that what I'm doing is good for you."

My mother hadn't scarfed much of the fry, and I figured it were 'cause she were struggle'n' with the sitch. I dealt bad and volunteered to red and wash dishes. My mother flashed in recognition that she knowed I were comprehend'n' and kind and proclaimed she were to soak in a bath. I quick red and, with my mother soak'n', I fisted the duffle from the room and tossed cans of soup and tuna from the cabinet and protein bars from the snack drawer. Loaded with supplies, I toted the duffle to the garage and dumped the food into the underseat cavity. I set the seat and strapped the duffle now containing just clothes. When my mother were plop'n' to eye TV, I were plop on the bed like nothing. I located to the TV room and plopped 'side my mother. We eyed a sitcom, and my mother unbraided my hair, combed it, and rebraided it. She facted that I'd RQ to learn care for long hair and braid tech, but that present, she'd aid. With hair freshly braided, I snuggled 'gainst the side of my mother, and she armed 'round me. A police procedural my mother flavored hit and for a while I were zoned and non-cognizant, a mere tyke lean'n' 'gainst a mother. I believe that my mother dismissed trouble for a sec too, and she gently rubbed her palm on my upper arm as we quietly eyed the TV.

▲▼▲

The police procedural were a renegade dick who were always figure'n' out the sitch when no one could. I hardly ever eyed TV, and the show were clown. Why was this dick who resides in a shab studio with intermittent web access figure'n' out crimes that the whole city heat couldn't untangle? And why were there numerous of these wack crimes? Were serial knifers drape'n' gym socks over victims and dudes obsessed with munch'n' fingers of forty year men really strut'n' all 'cross Manhattan? 'cord'n' to TV logic, ritual satan worship wacks and deranged Yoga instructors were the typical residents of the Big Apple. My mother were better at merely allow'n' dump to entertain and not over cogitate'n'. I were my father. He'd chuck when, with no plug, TV people ripped handguns in a tight hallway. "There goes another eardrum," he'd quib. I suppose he learnt me to question the real of the dump I eyed on screens. My mother didn't tolerate the TV real and would order us to walk. She'd creed everything don't have to correlate with real, that it were to entertain, not to cause no reflection. Present tense, I cogitate that my mother's step were on beat. I remain over-cogitate'n' and over-analyze'n'—that lump who fails to suspend disbelief. So there it is. As if I RQ to repeat myself, but I do 'cause of all the social contra. I ain't make believe'n'. I were a girl and then I were not. I lambed the pig and I flamed the cabin and they were both real which is something you'll eye as I return to the tell.

▲ ▼ ▲

But suspend disbelief, I don't camp there. Ever since all this girl/boy drop, I seem to twin the private dick and I ain't stumbled the master key but it ain't drugs or libation or make-believe or grief. I'm spill'n' that fact. Present, I burn sevens dust'n' clues and is all in on figure'n' this out. It's all stones to flip what I is presently, and tho I at times take it easy, I mostly scratch trees and bust boxes investigate'n'. My mother's 'bility to easy TV were how my mother easily 'cept me transformed to girl. She rationaled that it were a byproduct of drugs. She were the private dick with the easy master key—case closed. She didn't have no waiver in her conclusion. She hit a master key and eyed nothing more to eye. 'stead of son, she had daughter. Tho spontaneous transformations were certainly not regular, like the mystery that the TV dick eyed, neither she nor the TV dick questioned why the world were like this. They 'cepted it were the way it were.

▲ ▼ ▲

The show closed and I hit my room and texted Jessica till I 'eared my mother shut down. Jessica were grow'n' impatient and she were all questions 'bout the sitch. She were urge'n' to drop by and eye me. She claimed she missed me and was worried that I were 'bout break'n' us. Tho I 'tempted to reassure, she 'cused withhold'n' and deception and that were push'n' her insecure and frustrated. Eventually, I popped her GTG and that it were sad facts. She text-questioned what were sad facts. I ghosted.

▲ ▼ ▲

I knowed there were no cell at the cabin and that if I did tote my phone, its locale could be pinned, so I shut it and slid it in the desk drawer. No more connect with my group nor Jessica. It were then—as I hit all I were dump'n'—that tears actually realed. I bawled. I fisted frustration and Heinz 57ed at God. I silently cursed him for crush'n' this. Hadn't he 'ready thrown bricks? Weren't it someone else's turn to shaft? But after the bawl'n', the Heinz 57 settled into a general sadness. I reckoned that nothing had flipped—nothing were different. I were still solo, and I still had no option but to skedaddle. God silenced, just as God silenced when my father were cancer. I sometimes wonder how many times, in hits of desperation, that even the hardest atheist is tempted to cogitate that there is some force who can master it. How often do we pray this force to be a fixer—to untangle the knot, to solve the sitch, to cure the ill—only to be ignored. Social spewed recent that the universe is brick, and that if we all kicked, the universe would simply keep on spin'n'. The entire don't RQ us—we RQ it. Maybe that's why we desperately want it to dance, to bear us and spew us it is all roll'n' smooth. But like a kicked father, the universe ain't catch'n' no one. Fact, it don't even know that we RQ it. Philo for a sec: we ain't never outgrown the desire for the universe to nurture. We sprout and eventually realize that our actual parents are just loon lumps like us—fallible and struggle— with the same yearn for nurture from the eternal parent. And like us, they are bricked. My father must have stung this slap when he finally realized that he were cancer. He too must have hit God to aid—to flip better, to intercede— and like me, he must have hit brick. Did the brick make him Heinz 57? Did he despair? That I won't know. I imagine he gradually 'cepted the brick, he gradually 'cepted the silent, that, as he neared, he hit peace with the brick; yet, he were more religious than me and maybe he did 'ear God's voice, maybe God did nurture. Maybe I hit brick 'cause I have no god-relation. If that is, then that is; and if I have to do something different in order for the universe to spill, I've got no idea. If a kicked father and transformed girl ain't 'nough to pop the universe's eye, I'm creed'n' that I ain't interested in catch'n' them fish. End philo.

Att: Therapeutic Kate: I just did the philo to fact that I've pondered and I ain't just pop'n' pills hallucinate'n'. And that's facts to take to the bank.

▲ ▼ ▲

With a silent universe eye'n', I collected my cog, dried my tears, and 'tempted to cut the pity party. Certainly, I were forced to skedaddle. Certainly, stay'n' were a closed-door option. I knowed entire: I were strut in my father's shoes. He didn't want to cancer, he didn't want to kick, to abandon, to skedaddle; he were coerced. That parallel comforts some and builds strong. I washed my face, laced my sneakers, and slipped out. I hit the garage thru the side, disconnected the Genie and manual hefted the overhead to minimize the noise. I knowed the overhead up would 'lert suspicious in the AM, but I were feared that lower'n' would push luck. I opted to leave it up. I coasted the scooter to the street. The PM were dark and humid, and I could odor the 'proach of rain. It were not the ideal PM for a skedaddle on a vintage scooter, but it were what it were. I walked the scooter a block 'fore I figured it were safe to fire it. It RQD several kicks and play'n' the choke like a trombone to punch the old motor to alive, but persistence paid and the scooter fired 'bout the time that I were fatigue from kicks.

When I had fired it early it hadn't 'curred to eye the battery which were doornail. I knowed that scooters didn't RQ a battery for fire'n', but that the battery were power for the headlight and with a doornail battery, the scooter's headlight lit like a birthday candle and didn't do nothing to spot the road. Since it were past mid, there weren't no traffic, and I figured if I were careful, I could ride out of town. By the time I'd hit to the rural, I hoped the battery would regain sufficient to flash the headlight. If not, I would have to hunker till the AM hit bright 'nough to ride sans headlight. Either way, I knowed I RQD miles 'tween me and the house 'fore my mother uncovered I were skedaddled. I hit off down the road slow and steady.

'bout halfway out of town, the headlamp turned up a few candles 'cause the motor charged the drain, but a new sitch hit—the PM started to drop rain. First it were simple mist and I were capable of negotiate'n' thru, but as the rain intensed, it quickly washed in my eyes and visibility were near nothing. I were forced to park under a bridge and plop till it lessened. As the rain splat the empty road, I center-standed the scooter and cut the motor. I dismounted and posted at the edge of the underpass and eyed the rain thru dim moonlight. It were sort of a peace and calm experience. The moon caused the scene to ink and reflected just 'nough off the damp pavement that I could eye splashes of drops collide'n'. A light breeze picked and cooled the air that the rain were rinse'n' of pollen and soot and sulfate. I 'eared a locomotive whistle and then the quiet rumble of freight trained 'cross the region. My mind went to wonder'n' 'bout the hobo and the vagabond who past tense jumped boxcars and railed 'cross states. When I were tyke, my father RQD me to eye a flick with him 'bout an Oakie guitar drift who railed trains like that. I didn't spark the flick or the wack's jams, but I did hit the hobo lifestyle solid. It 'curred that a lump had to be king-cock to reside like that—to just rail 'round and not fret future—to just figure it smooth, and altho I weren't rail'n' no train bound for nowhere, I were set on a vintage scooter, and, like a hobo, I were bridge-shelter'n' in the midst of a skedaddle.

Gradually the rain dialed to drizzle. I climbed back on the scooter—it fired easy now that it were 'custom—and I motored from under the bridge. I rode a half 60 or so 'fore stop'n' to fuel. I figured I could reach the cabin on one tank, but I were fret'n' that I'd have insufficient fuel to scamp anywhere else.

The gas station were dingy and poorly lit. I center-standed 'side one of two analog pumps, cut the motor and topped the tank. I dripped 40:1 in the tank like my father had learnt me and went to pay. 'fore I paid, I eyed a quick pass of the small store to discover if they might have goggles or something I could protect over my eyes while I rode. I knowed that glasses eased ride'n', but in my emotional departure, I hadn't cogitated 'bout no eyewear and had ridden thus squint 'gainst wind which dried my eyes. Plus, 'casionally, a bug or a grime speck directed at my pupil. The store displayed shades, and I opted on a pair with light lenses. I coined the glasses and the fuel and, 'fore mount'n' the scooter, I hit the john. The toilet were grease stained and moldy, and there were blood splatters on the wash basin. I fished the shrunken and peed in the urinal which smelt of disinfect chemicals and sweat. I were forced to post uncomfortably tight to the filthy porcelain. Tho I 'tempted not to brush 'gainst the urinal, my thigh contacted the side. I recoiled and sprayed the wall 'fore I redirected. There were a crusty circular towel hung and the sink were too filthy to even consider. I had no foggy notion what had transpired in that john nor how long it were since it were serviced. Over the walls, previous perv lumps Sharpied penises and profanities and digits for encounters. There were a f-bomb at the president but I didn't care 'bout that 'cause I ain't political. Which is more facts that I ain't woke to nothing. This is mere auto-bio for Therapeutic Kate. It ain't a woke manifesto nor an anti-woke commentary. Contrary social claims is bogus. Jimmy V were the only lump I knowed who toted a Sharpie and he ain't political neither. He just tagged his signature penises. 'k, more diverge. but it's facts I weren't no Sharpie tagger. Even present tense I merely 'tempt to get thru 60 and then the next 60. Sharpie taggers were premeditated. The tags were spontaneous, but tote'n' a Sharpie were a conscious choice like tuck'n' a piece. Each were messages but Sharpie taggers were hit'n' the uncensored free-speech arena which is more than anyone can spill for the social wacks who is all 'bout likes and reposts. Sharpie taggers scribed bigoted propaganda 'side hippie peace signs, and drew bubbly unicorns with stiff penises. Sometimes I would eye close at Sharpie walls, but this john were more than typically filthy, and I 'turned to the store with nothing but a pass'n' glance at the tags. I remained disgusted from my thigh brush'n' the urinal, when I 'eared the clerk 'hind the counter question if I were one of them freaks. I stopped and turned to face. I must have 'peared puzzled 'cause he drew on a cig then flashed.

"Look, I don't care much myself, but it'd be better if you used the lady's toilet in the future."

'fore it registered that he cogitated girl, I questioned what he were spill'n'.

"Look, I'm just saying that if there happened to be a guy in the toilet and a sweet little thing like you walked in, well that guy might get the wrong idea."

He winked, exhaled stale cigarette smoke and questioned if that were what I were look'n' for. He must have cogitated he were go'n' to finally have a porno-perv event with a nympho in the 24/7.

The clerk were skinny and bony and his teeth were yellow. He had long stringy hair and skin that eyed like it would still be dirty even after a shower scrub. He wore a partially buttoned Hawaiian shirt and saggy blue jeans. He set on a stool behind plexi. He ground his spent cigarette into an ashtray, posted and walked toward the door that separated him from the customers. I sensed his porno-perv intents and bolted toward the exit. 'fore I made it, the clerk were out from 'hind the counter and block'n'.

"Come on honey, what ya looking for tonight?"

I clutched a quart of Valvoline from a shelf and hurled it at his face. It missed and bounced off the door. That seemed to fire the clerk more excited as he flashed large.

"So you're a feisty one. No need to be ashamed here, honey. We both know what you want; you don't have to pretend that I'm forcing you."

The second quart of oil whacked square 'cross his face. That made him Heinz 57 and he lunged at me.

"Fuck, you want it rough? Fine, let's play rough."

He grabbed for my arm. I spun 'way from his grip and backed down the aisle as he slowly pursued me like a gauge'n' bear. The aisle were not long and at the end were a high stack of Bud 12s. I busted them over and cans popped and sprayed beer 'cross the floor cause'n' a general commotion. The perv slipped when he re-lunged and smashed hard on his shoulder. I were full Heinz 57 myself. This perv were 'tempt'n' to porno-perv me and screw that. So with the perv face-floored, I booted his head like a rocket PT. His face concaved and blood mingled with beer suds. I cocked for a second PK, but my left knee caved and I faced the tile. The perv gripped my foot and hoisted me toward. I palmed up a loose Bud and pelted it at his head. The can near missed, but exploded when it floored. Beer sprayed and the pressure shot the can 'cross the tile. I rolled and slipped my foot from his grip. I hurled another Bud can at him. It bounced off his skull and geysered. I scrambled to my feet and PKed him a solid to the ribs 'fore I door-bolted. The perv were still scramble and full porno-perv. I knowed I would not have time to kick the scooter, so, I pulled the nozzle from the pump and locked the handle in the open. Fuel sprayed from the hose. I dropped the handle and mounted the scooter. The perv 'tempted to off the flail nozzle. By the time he had the shut off, the scooter were kicked to life. I motored out to the dark road. For twenty yards or so the perv hit after. When it were crystal that I were 'celerate'n', he uncled and spewed dribble that I couldn't clearly 'ear. I were beer and gasoline washed and knowed I'd be in boil'n' water if the perv opted to ring the heat. All he had to spill were that a wack-bag ransacked his store and spewed gasoline over the place, and I'd be roast. If the heat didn't immediate cage me, they would at least ring my mother who probably would let me rot the PM in the cell and then spring me in the AM. She'd bust the scooter and be on high alert for other skedaddle 'tempts and there I'd be in a jumper and blouse learn'n' 'bout triangles at Our Lady of Perpetual Sorrows.

A tick tweaked my shoulder as I hit back out on the road and realized what danger I had actually divested. I certainly were not at my stone strong and that perv most likely would have powered me. The visual of him palm'n' me shocked another jolt 'cross my shoulder. What would he have done? I tried not to visualize, but images of this perv force pornoperv'n' me, of him body palm'n', of his surprise or maybe delight at the discovery of what were down below washed my mind. Acid rose in the back of my throat and, as visions of the perv porn-perv'n' me drenched my mind, the scooter's front tire dropped in a winter pothole and I spilled.

The pavement were still damp, and I weren't go'n' at speed. Aside from scraped palms, I examined myself unijured and the scooter unscarred. I were know'n' 'bout my new body and knowed that I RQD to close-eye for injury that I might not have first noticed. I visualed my smashed fingers and my gashed bicep. I had numbed those. I patted down every area of my body that I could reach and all checked normal. The spill momentarily jared the porno-perv out of my head, and, as I remounted, I shifted focus to the road and, as my father had learnt me, to eye far forward and 'ticipate hazard, debris, and critter. He preached this was the numero uno for a clean ride. The dos were that the scooter goes where the head is eye'n'. If you wanted to ditch, he'd pontificate, eye at the ditch and that's where you'll wind.

Cogitate'n' 'bout that settled me but then the violent 'curred. In full Heinz 57, I'd rocket PKed that perv twice. That he remained pursuant meant I were not rock 'cause I normally slam. Not be'n' rock were plus/minus. If I were rock and full face pked the perv, he'd be slack. I had been full Heinz 57 'fore, but always restrained to dish'n' a blood nose or a soft PK in a gut, but never were I not cogitate 'bout when to halt. But with this perv, I would have smashed him doornail and then really been up the river. And here I spill this anecdote 'cause it's contra that I run violent and that I were on a tri-state spree. Facts is I were just piss'n' and the perv tried to porno-perv me and that's like the pig too, but we'll hit that later.

Like anyone, I get Heinz 57, but I ain't perpetual Heinz 57. Jessica could 'test to that, but she's emo-reject and punch'n' the like on anti-social and there ain't nothing like a woman scorned. The perv never rang the heat and no one bothered to track him to creed this. He probably flew south and is porno-perv'n' in a roadside 24/7 or BJ'n' a truck stop. For cert he ain't crack'n' this therapeutic 'cause he's a perv and probably ashamed of the service-beat he took from a girl. Funny that he don't know the face-rocket PK were from a less than rock boy or probably he'd feel redemption. K, more diverge, but RQD diverge and that's facts.

▲ ▼ ▲

In the Chrysler, my father could haul to the cabin in under 90, but I weren't exact of the locale of the cabin. I knowed the general, but I couldn't motor major roads 'cause I didn't have no power to compete with the rigs and Cadillacs. Even if so, I still would have avoided majors on the off that the heat might eye suspicious and barrier me. This fear were intensed by the possibility that the perv might have rung the heat. So I diverted lowkey cross backs aimed north or east. I realized that I didn't have to show at the cabin at any particular, so diverge'n' on these desolate backs 'peared like the ace option.

Eventually the PM transitioned into AM and when morn broke, I eyed that the day were overcast and threat'n' 'dditional rain. I had diverged so many backs that I weren't exact how near I were to the cabin, but I desired arrival 'fore the rain. I 'mained the back I were on for twenty 'fore it finally intersected with a state that I knowed would wind to the cabin. It were a major, and I should not have been motor'n' a vintage scooter on it, but I diced it so as to short the sojourn. I mained the shoulder and concentrated to diverge debris and chunks of tar pavement. Three times rigs blew by. The gust from the rigs would shake me and brief suck me toward the tires 'fore it would dissipate quick for me to recover balance. The ride were harrow and I were grateful to spin off onto the county road that hit to the cabin before the heat or a rig barricaded.

The county road were bad. Potholes and crumbled patches of pavement dominated. It were difficult to cogitate anything other than a full redo would ever repair the surface to smooth. I slowed so much that I RQD to post my legs out to stop from tip'n'. Eventually I eyed the farm house I were seek'n' and localed the rutted path to the cabin. The path were overgrown with long grass and weed. Honeysuckle had also knotted 'cross cause'n' anything but a scooter a difficult passage. I were relieved to eye the path neglected and forgotten and hoped that meant that the cabin would be an inconspicuous sanctuary.

I maneuvered the path till the cabin came in. It 'peared tight shut and, as I had hoped, clearly lost in the shuffle of cancer and the details 'round my father's kick'n'. I centerstanded the scooter 'tween two mature trees that umbrellaed the cabin. I walked the perimeter to assure that the place were deserted. The shutters were closed and secured and the front and back doors were pad-locked. There were no indication of foot traffic nor worn paths from or to. I breathed relief and then walked up on the front porch. I tilted the log that my father utilized as a side table and slipped the padlock key.

The cabin were musty and damp and it were obvious that no one had occupied recently. I propped the front and un-

barred the back to allow some air. The day remained overcast and the early spring were chill, yet the outside subdued
the musty dampness. I retrieved my duffle and supplies and
walked 'round the cabin unlatch'n' the shutters and shutter
dog'n' them open. Inside I lifted the windows. It didn't rain
for several 60s and the cabin had a chance to air 'fore I shut
the windows and the back. During those first few 60s, I
should have ignited a fire and better prepped for the PM, but
I fatigued and soon crashed deep on top of the damp bed'n'.
I woke with shivers. It were hard rain'n' and densely black.

That first PM were ice and soak. Past tense, whoever constructed the cabin knocked hard-wood logs for walls,
chinked with mud, clay and whatever else were convenient,
and split red cedar shakes for roof'n'. When my father reclaimed, he knocked the old chink and replaced it with Port-
land cement. Originally there were no glass, just rectangle
open'n's that could be plank shuttered. My father salvaged
wood windows from a farm he listed and, with leftover
chink, he wangled them into the spaces. He shuttered and
latched when he vacated to prevent lumps from stumble'n'
upon and bust'n' the glass. He pontificated that there were
something 'bout unbroken glass in secluded structures that
pulled vandals like a left out watermelon pulled ants. The
shake roof presented the big hitch. The shakes RQD mainte-
nance and often replacement. A pile of them stacked knee-
high and four 'cross fulled the corner of the out-shed behind.
I once questioned my father if the shed originated as an out-
house. He mottoed that for guys, all nature were a toilet. My
father often labored on the shake roof, only to stay one fix
behind the drips. When a drip drip drip would spatter the
table, my father would rise early AM, ladder the roof with an
arm of shakes, a hammer and a pouch of nails. He'd figure
guess faulty shakes, pry them loose and nail new ones in.
Times he'd descend down, butane a tar bucket, ladder the
bucket up and splash tar 'cross areas that 'peared, even after
new shakes, particularly prone to drips. He'd ladder down
satisfied that the final drip were pinched only to 'ear, during

the next heavy rain, the familiar drip drip drip—this time over the mantle indicate'n' faulty flashing.

No one had landed at the cabin in over three years by my estimation and, in that time, sans my father's fixes and maintains, the drips had overtook. I found it difficult to even locale one completely dry spot to plop. The hard steady rain pounded all thru my crash, and intermittent into the early 60s of the AM. The roof worked more like a colander than a barrier and the rain dripped in so many spots that bucket and saucepan collect'n' eventually pointed futile. The plank floor were most soaked and many of the boards were slightly warped. Everything in the cabin, include'n' me, were soggy. I 'tempted to hang my duffle dry on the coat rack, but a drip sprung unnoticed and eventually the bag watered heavy with wet clothes and shoes and tilted the coat rack off balance and crashed.

To make it worse, it were a cold rain, and I shivered thru as I plopped the soggy bed wrapped in three wool blankets and a blue plastic tarp that I stole off a pile of wood stacked 'gainst the back of the cabin. The cabin didn't have no electric nor propane nor nothing like that. When it chilled, my father burnt in the big stone fireplace, and he cooked on an old cast iron stove. The stove originally drew heat from coal, but he found if he chopped wood to small chunks he could generate 'nough heat to boil eggs, filet a fish from the Allegheny or fry some meat if he stepped lucky and popped a rabbit. When I finally got 'round 'tempt'n' to light fire, the matches had damped and didn't spark. Sans fire, I huddled in a dark shiver till I eventually crashed back asleep.

I awoke to eye a fresh world. Thru the window glass, 'tempt'n' to dry and warm the place, bright yellow rays of sunshine beamed. I peeled the tarp and wool blankets and the entire of my damp clothes. Naked, I posted, hefted the bottom sash of the near window, unlatched the shutters and pushed them open. The shutters clapped the exterior of the cabin, and it 'curred to me that if I were eye'n' from the vantage of the woods, I would be peep'n' a naked girl at an open window, arms spread and girl tits full on. The cognate hit me self-conscious but then I minded that in all the every I had landed here with my father, we had never had any pop-guests or thru-hikers rap'n' the door eye'n' for grub or water. I blocked open the back to allow more sun and warmth in, lifted the windows, and then walked out onto the porch expose'n' my skin to the rays. The thick braid my mother had woven my hair into laid uncomfortable and soggy. I reached the end off my back and eyed it for a time 'fore cogitate'n' the complexity of the weave that locked the ends. After much fiddle'n', I eventually freed my hair and shook it out. It stranged to shook out long hair from a braid, and I finger raked and 'tempted to untangle and straighten the hair. Even tho my lower were shrunken and obscured, I peed off the side of the porch. I then rotated so the sun could warm the whole front of me. For the first in seven, I hit an iota of calm. All seemed exactly where it were supposed to be and all hit harmony. I cogitated my choir class at Sacred Heart. Mr. DeLudovico were always 'tempt'n' to blend us to harmony. We would 'tempt, but we always flunked it wrong, and DeLudovico would wave us off till we all shamed and bowed our heads. He'd spin the Beach Boys *I Get Around* and The Beatles *Don't Let Me Down* and tear when he 'eared the beauty of the harmony.

"This isn't just random magic. Harmony comes when notes combine into chords. Think of each voice as a separate note of a major chord. When sung correctly, the chord rings. That is harmony. When it happens, and it doesn't happen often, the singers experience a spiritual oneness that some describe as transcendent."

Our choir ain't never achieved transcendence or if it did, it 'curred sans me. I never souled what Mr. DeLudovico were spill'n' 'bout. Maybe others popped, but I gutted 'lone and separate. I soloed. No barbershop for me. It weren't my ride. I ever differed, and once my father kicked, the differ-voice amped 'cause I 'came the wack with the kicked father. Yet, aside from all that, post'n' there naked with my girl body, with the warmth of the sun flood'n' over me, with the chirp'n' birds, the frolic'n' squirrels, the absolute still of the air, the lilac scent mixed with the aroma of evaporate'n' rain and soggy detritus, all were unite and for the first time in my life, I 'stood what it popped like to harmony—merely to fold in, to uncle resist and fight and single out, to mesh and blend. The pop only durationed a few 'fore the sun 'came too warm and 'fore self-conscious 'bout be'n' naked and out-doors dropped me out.

▲▼▲

There weren't much I could fix 'bout my nakedness 'less I donned soggy clothes which I weren't. On whatever would serve as a rack, I spread all my clothes to dry. Then I com-menced the arduous task of clean'n' and organize'n' the cab-in. I knowed I would eventually need to address the drip roof, but I were not go'n' to ladder nude. The sun made it 'ppear that it wouldn't rain 'gain for ages, and I figured I had ample to 'tempt the roof drips after my clothes dried and I had red and organized the inner of the cabin.

By combin'n several collection dishes, I were able to half fill two buckets with rain from the drip roof and utilized one 'long with an old rag to wipe the surfaces. I draped the blan-kets and bed coverings over the front railing, and edge post-ed the mattress. A gentle warm breeze hit up and entered thru the open windows and door and gradually things began to dry. In a cupboard, I found matches that weren't soggy, and I managed to ignite a fire in the stove and the hearth. I toted in armloads of wood and piled them near the stove and the fireplace so to fast dry. I poured the water from the other bucket into an old dutch oven that were set on the battered drop-leaf table. I relocated it to the stove to boil. Once the drip boiled, I could cool it and then safely drink. In a mili-tary-surplus footlocker, I localed cans of soup, four sealed containers stuffed with deer jerky, a flashlight with decent batteries, two more wool blankets, a few pairs of hunting socks, some bandanas, a box of 12 gauge shells, a large filet knife and a worn paperback of Zen sayings called *Just Be*.

By the time I had drinkable water, a relative clean and dry habitat, and some vittles, it were hit'n' late afternoon. I checked my clothes. They were stiff dry. I folded them best I could and stacked them on a bench under a window. I slid into a pair of athletic pants and the Liverpool FC jersey, but, after coast'n' the day naked, the clothes felt restrict'n', and I stripped them. A broom leaned in the corner and for the next two 60s I broomed and re-broomed the plank floor. Eventually, there were not even anything to broom, but the broom'n' hit satisfy, and I remained it. I imagined that the cabin had never been so broomed, and I continued till my arms fatigued. I spotted the bedding which remain draped over the porch rail. It were dry and the mattress also were dry. I dropped the mattress flat and spread the covers. With the fire, the floor freshly broomed and the cabin generally red and aired, it homed and comforted. Nothing were left to do but repair the drip roof which I had opted to an AM task.

On the floor in front of the fireplace, I plopped on a blanket and stared at the flame. Soon, like worms burrow'n' into an apple, thoughts crept my head. I found myself re-wonder'n' why I were a girl, why my mother, Father Antonio, and even Dr. Phillips didn't creed I weren't slop'n' no drugs. I wondered what were to 'come of my life, my start on the soccer team, Jessica. Were pervs eye'n' for me? How long could I sanctuary here till it 'curred to someone that I might be localed at my father's cabin? What if 'nother perv popped with a blade and porno-perv intents. I were only a girl for a short and there were the hospital perv and then the 24/7 gas perv. When I were boy I eyed porn to pop off and maybe I were a bit perv, but I weren't force porno-perv. At least I didn't cogitate I were. But I were the hand one with Jessica and she were the resist. I'd hit as far as she were open. Maybe she didn't joy that. Maybe she wished I'd just stop hit'n' at every opportunity and just palm hands and eye stares. It were entirely confuse'n' and I had managed to distract by the red'n' and broom'n' and dry'n', but now it were all hard and cold fact. I usually didn't pray, but, with eye-tears and a hard-beat heart, I kneed, touched hands together in front of my girl tits and prayed what Father Antonio would call a *false* prayer. I prayed that God would make things different—that my body would go back to boy, that all would spin out into a bizarre dream—but prayer don't operate like that. Not only did Father Antonio mind us of that in religion, so did Sister Mary Beth who made us hand spew an essay 'bout the time Huck Finn didn't get the fish hooks he prayed for. I stopped skim'n' that book a few chapters later when Sister Mary Beth spoiled by spill'n' that the kicked lump in the float'n' house were Huck's dad. Sister Mary Beth were 'tempt'n' us to cogitate 'bout Jim's humanity. She pontificated that Mark Twain were the original American author to ink a slave character who were human, that Jim's cover were one of the hints that Jim were IQ and strategic. She cogitated that we'd care, but nowadays we's all know black lumps are the same as white lumps and so course Jim wouldn't spill to Huck. Who would? Huck were Jim's ticket. Any white lump in Jim's shoes would have done the same. So with my mind concluded, I stopped skim'n' and utilized notes from a senior who had sat previous. In the comments she inked at the end of the plagiarized junk that I were an insightful young man and that all I RQD to do were apply. She pontificated that I were more twin to Huck than I realized, and she doodled a smiley face. The nuns at Sacred Heart were all 'tempt'n' to lean on relationships due to a Catholic initiative emphasize'n' compassion, but facts is they were all ghost-fake, and altho a few of my group felt like there were some confide nuns, I skepticaled.

Prayer would be solid if God considered what a lump were request'n' and then sometimes decided that the lump had a good point and POOF changed the world to 'commodate. Maybe some wretch would suddenly nail the lotto after pray'n' for relief, or some gimp would suddenly run a track star after recite'n' ten Our Fathers, or maybe I would even 'turn boy with a live mother and a live father. Yet, Sister Mary Beth and Father Antonio and I guess Mark Twain knowed that there were better reasons to pray and maybe it were that prayer makes us cogitate. Here I were front of a warm fire, naked and kneed and my initial request that God turn my life to normal just spiraled into cognition 'bout Huck Finn and platitudes Sister Mary Beth scrawled at the end of an essay that I most copied. Maybe cogitate and pray were synonymous and maybe that's what Father Antonio were pontificate'n' when he creeded we pray to change us not to change God. Prayer should be like cogitate'n' 'bout our dump and figure'n' it 'stead of ask'n for a bailout. That felt spot, but it also felt blue. I were only sixteen; my father were kicked and my body were girl. A vivid of my father popped in my head. He were in a coffin flash'n' at me. Tears hit. I might be able to red and broom; I might even be able to repair the drip-roof; I might be able to momentarily sanctuary, but like drips find'n' the cracks, my kicked father and my girl body were always gonna seep thru little open'n's that I'd not never completely seal. With tears still, my core quit, and I planted to my side. My arm extended to prop and my legs bent under. I could usually kneel for duration without support due to daily condition'n' exercises. The coach whistled us in and spewed it were prayer time. We'd drop knees, suck in guts and straighten backs. We posed for five minutes 'less the coach were Heinz 57 and he'd hit us prayer-pose for ten. As my body adjusted to girl, my rock and athletic gradually returned. I figured the initial numbness and clumsiness were part of the transition, but now I started to wonder if maybe something else were 'cur'n'. I had rocked solid all day, but then, on my knees to pray, my core quit, and I toppled like soggy toast.

It RQD me several minutes to regain rock, and, once I did, it RQD all my spunk to post and make it to the bed where I plopped under the bedding and quickly crashed.

▲▼▲

The AM I woke 'gain to bright sun. I had quick-crashed into bed without shut'n' windows nor doors and the sun were take'n' advantage of ease entry. The windows were screened and my father had hinged a screen door so he could open the place up and remain deter of mosquitoes and the infiltration of squirrels, skunks, opossums and whatever else might odor food.

I slowly rose and checked rock and stability. The fatigue were lifted and my girl body naturally coordinated and rocked. I drank some water, chawed some jerky and opted to ladder on the roof and address the drips when I were still rock. I didn't know if or when I might relapse into a pile of sand, but I didn't desire to spend another PM in a cabin that, during rain, doubled as a shower head. I pulled on my athletic pants and Liverpool jersey, slid some socks over my feet and tied my sneakers. It still felt odd to be restricted up, but even tho I were in the hard rural, modest decorum dictated I cover my nakedness.

There were a gray wood ladder leant 'gainst the woodpile. I sat the ladder 'gainst the back roof, went to the shed where I collected several shakes, a hammer and a nail pouch which I cinched 'round my waist. I figured I'd ladder up and eye for cracks or AWOL shakes and replace those first, then, if it necessitated, I'd flame the tar bucket, ladder it up the roof, and drizzle tar anywhere that eyed like it might be a drip spot. I labored till late afternoon replace'n' shakes and drizzle'n' tar. The more shakes I replaced, the more I eyed ones suspicious. I'm certain I replaced many shakes that were solid, but once I commenced bust'n' worn and nail'n' down new, ten more old ones suddenly awared and RQD replacement. When I forced myself to stop tear'n' out and replace'n', I fired the tar bucket and drizzled tar in all conceivable crevices and cracks. Black tar splat my sneakers and my athletic pants and some of it glued to my hands. When I laddered down final, sat the tar bucket on the ground to cool and laid the ladder, my hands were most black and my sneakers and athletic pants were ruined.

I stripped and abandoned the tar cake clothes on the ground 'side the back. I would dispose of them future tense. I had eyed my father strip tar from his hands with polysorbate that he stowed in the first aid. I localed it, slapped the cream and let it soak for several 'fore I 'tempted to wipe. It took four applications, but eventually my hands were most tar free.

As I reached to return the cream to the first aid in the upper cupboard, I 'eared a metallic tap whenever my left foot posted the floor. I sat down, pulled my foot up on my thigh and eyed a roofing nail impaled in the heel. I must have stepped it when I were strip'n' the splattered shoes and athletic pants. The nail were hilted with the broad head serve'n' as cork. I suspected that once I pried the nail, blood would wine from the puncture. I tore a large gauze pad and rummaged a roll of white medical from the first aid. I gripped the nail out and tighted the gauze against the hole. I fumbled with the tape and eventually secured the gauze. It were then that it 'curred that I had doctored this like I were aid'n' someone else. I felt no pain. Fact, I felt no sensation in my foot at all. I stomped my foot and then posted. Nada. No sensory. I lifted my other foot and balanced with weight full on the injury. Still no sensory, nada. This must be identical to my gash arm. For some unexplained, specifics of my body were numb. I grabbed a fork from a drawer and sat back at the drop-leaf. Gently, I commenced poke'n'. I started at my head, my face and even my tongue. Everything from neck up hit normal. My shoulders too were register'n' sensation, but patches of my arms and hands were completely numb. It turned out the same were facts with my legs and feet. I poked 'round my gut and even a bit at my girl tits. Everything sensed there. For obvious, I avoided the shrunken down. Conclusion were random areas of arms, legs, hands, and feet were sensory dead. This explained the impaled nail and the arm gash. I found a Sharpie in a drawer and circled areas that sensed numb. I don't know why that impulse 'curred to me. Maybe I wanted to science if there would be new sensory numb down the road, or maybe I just wanted to certain carefully not to maim these spots since they were dead. I imagine I eyed silly-nilly with black circle tattoos random on my extremities, but it 'peared right, so I arted it.

The sun half set by the time I ended the ink'n'. I roused the embers in the cook stove, added some wood chunks, and timed for the stove to activate enough to warm a soup can. While the soup heated, I blazed the fire in the hearth and slid into a fresh pair of athletic pants. The gauze on my foot were red but not saturated so I figured that maybe the bleeding had staunched. After ladle'n' out some soup, I propped my injured foot on a chair, eyed the fire, and slurped the soup. I forewent with grace which I knowed would have riled my mother, but mindless recitation 'fore grub never made no sense, and I only recited to 'pease her. Present tense, solo in my father's cabin, I freed. If I desired prayer or grace, I could, but no one were there to compulse. I didn't have to pantomime or post line to 'pease my mother or Father Antonio. Least that segment of this solo felt aces. I soon found myself cogitate'n' 'bout what else might be aces 'bout this solo. My father optimized and fancied to figure what were aces dressed as tens. When 9/11 blew, he gloried the united it caused and the outpour aide for the victims. When my soccer team gravelled a match, he'd question what I learnt from the punk, pontificate'n' that gravel were more aid than pavement. He even localed the up in his cancer creed'n' that most lumps carry on like they's got ample time and then one day they wake up kicked. A terminal diagnosis were 'minder that time is a walled diamond. Facts clichéd, he scribed a bucket and actually Xed off all 'cept trod'n' up Mount Kilimanjaro and eye'n' me diploma.

▲ ▼ ▲

'sides not recitation prayers 'fore grub, I 'minded that I also were localed in my father's cabin and that hit familiar and calm. My father and I had burned many weekends in this cabin and altho I often slumped 'bout be'n' 'way from my group and that the cabin were sans internet nor cell, I also sorta 'joyed the temporary shut down. Fish'n' and hunt'n' and wander'n' 'round the woods were acts that most of my group didn't do and acts that I hit exclusive solo with my father. My mother had only localed to the cabin once and that were back when my father had pretty much ended clink'n' it habitable and desired her to eye it. My mother complimented him that he'd done a spot job hit'n' the place present. She gifted a crucifix and instructed him to hang it and then she posted that she were ready for home. He motored her home and, to my know, she never re-localed the place. My father often hit it, and, as I oldered, he toted me 'long. One of the first things we did during those early locales was treble-hook catfish in the Allegheny. I'll not forget the first I reeled one in. It felt like I had snagged a bowl'n' ball and my father flashed as I fought the thing. It turned out a three pound ugly old flathead—speck with dull golden and dark green splotches. Its barbels hung from 'round its wide flat mouth like long flimsy spikes. My father had to plier out the treble 'cause I feared to palm the thing. He proclaimed it a mighty good catch tho and proclamated we were go'n' to grub good that PM. He plumped the ugly thing into a five gallon that he had part filled with Allegheny. We stowed up our gear and hit back to the cabin. There were a stump out back that my father utilized to clean fish. He sent me to rummage the filet knife and when I returned my father were palm'n' the fish flat on the stump. He learnt me how to slit the top of the fish and then where to slice to filet. I did a reasonable wack job hack'n' that flathead, but over time, I developed as fast as my father and either of us could filet a cat in less than a minute. That first fish got breaded and fried on the cookstove. While we grubbed, my father folklored that his dad would drain the blood out of catfish by hang'n' them and chop'n' their tails. He laughed and claimed that if the fish weren't all the way kicked when you lopped its tail, it'd flip jump all over spray'n' blood guts till it finally bled out.

I cogitated 'bout fish'n' with my father as I slurped spoonfuls of soup. When the bowl were nearly empty, I tilted the remains into my mouth and thought how 'palled my mother would be at my manners. I were careful to post and test my sturdy as I rose and toted the bowl and spoon to the counter. I gulped water from a galvanized water urn that I had loaded with boil-water earlier AM, and with nothing to hit, I flipped the bandage on my foot and slid into bed. It had been a long day of drip repair and I quickly crashed into dreamless black.

▲ ▼ ▲

"Well, well, well, look what the cat dragged in."

I sprung to eye who were proclamate'n'. The covers fell off expose'n' my girl tits.

"Hey there, you'd better cover those before someone gets the wrong impression."

The man were emaciated and miss'n' several teeth. He wore jeans that eyed like he hadn't washed them or even removed them from his body in ages. His tee and rat flannel were faded tawny and they seemed to blend into one. He had a broken open shotgun in the crook of his arm and a tattered duffle hung on his shoulder. His hair and beard were long strands of gray and black. He could have been fifty or ninety.

I clutched the blanket and covered myself. A shiver-tremble hit as the thought 'curred that this lump were also a perv and were 'bout to lamb me, porno-perv me, or both.

"You must be Goldilocks?"

The man flashed a wheeze-laugh.

"Which makes me Papa Bear. I hope the bed wasn't too hard for you."

He lifted eyebrows and wheeze-laughed repeat.

I burrowed a bit deeper into the blankets as if they could shield. I were fear but slightly Heinz 57 too. I eyed the filet knife but it were 'cross over on the counter and the lump posted 'tween.

"Is my little Goldilocks afraid? Relax, I'm just messing with you. It's not everyday that I find a naked girl sleeping in this cabin, so excuse me for playing around."

I held silent and still like a paint'n' and eyed the filet knife.

"My name's Tumult. What's yours?"

I eyed at him with lowered eyebrows.

"Tumult?"

His flash showed his miss'n' and chipped teeth. He eyed like he'd a few times been a homerun baseball.

"Yep, I go by Tumult. Now, who do I have the pleasure of talking to?"

Tumult odored rank and sour. I masked the comforter over my nose.

"Whatta ya want?"

The Heinz 57 were out wrestle'n' the fear.

"What do I want? Why child, I just want to know what you're called."

"You're trespass'n' and my father's got a Winchester that'll out gun that shotgun so maybe you oughta move 'long 'fore he comes back."

"Comes back? Back from where?"

"He's rabbit hunt'n'. Due back any time now."

"Now that's a trick I'd pay to see. A dead man shooting a rabbit. And for my next illusion..."

Tumult flashed and wheezed.

I shuttered that he knowed 'bout my father but figured he could be guess'n'.

"Did you shoot my father? Are you gonna shoot me?"

"Did I shoot your father? What nonsense are you talking? You're a scared one, aren't you?"

I silenced and slit my eyes.

"Now look here. I ain't about to hurt no one. I'm just a visitor. How about you tell me your name? You know it's po- lite to introduce yourself and I'm sure your mother taught you manners."

"Paul Joseph. Satisfied? How 'bout you go 'way now?"

Tumult raised his eyebrows and straightened his back.

"Paul Joseph? Now isn't that a strange name for a girl."

"That's my name and I ain't a girl."

I proclamated into the comforter.

Tumult glanced the broken shotgun rest'n' in the crook of his arm. Then he eyed at me with his jagged-toothed grin.

"You ain't a girl?"

"No, I ain't."

"Well I suppose looks can be deceiving, but I'd put a hundred to one that those things on your chest belong to a girl."

I chose no response and eyed Heinz 57.

"Well if we're going to play it like that then I'm just going to call you Goldilocks."

"My name's Paul Joseph."

"Well Paul Joseph or Goldilocks, here's what's gonna happen. I'm gonna step out on the porch so you can put some clothes on and then the two of us are gonna have us a little chat."

"A chat? A chat 'bout what? Why are you here? This is my father's cabin."

"Well, is it now? I guess that'll be one item on our agenda."

Tumult turned and then hit out onto the porch. The screen door clapped, and he posted with his back to the cabin. I slipped from the covers, and then I pulled on a clean pair of athletic pants and the Liverpool jersey. The previous AM, I had 'tempted to ponytail my hair 'fore I laddered the roof, but I couldn't local anything to secure it back. 'stead, I dug a bandana out of the army foot and tied it 'round my head. The bandana were on the drop leaf. I finger-raked my hair back and then fixed the bandana on. It worked reasonably good at keep'n' the hair out of my face. I slid into my remain'n' pair of sneakers, careful not to bust the gauze wrap. 'fore I stepped out onto the porch, I palmed the filet knife from the counter and cut it under the mattress. It seemed like Tumult could be danger, and I might RQ to defend myself. If he porno-perved on me, I figured he pin me on the bed and I desired the filet in reach.

Clothed and with the stashed filet, I hit a bit comfort. I toed out onto the porch. Tumult faced. Post'n' next to him, he didn't seem large or intimidate'n' like when he were leer'n' over my bed and I were girl-naked under the covers. The day were sun and a bit breeze. I positioned upwind and 'gain shot Tumult why he were here at my father's cabin.

"No breakfast?"

"Breakfast?"

"I know your mother taught you to offer nourishment to visitors? What grub you got around this place?"

Before I replied, Tumult screen-doored. I followed. Like he knowed the place as good as me, he flipped the army foot and palmed a jerky pouch. He opened it and then bit a chunk. He walked to the counter, grabbed a tin and filled it with water from the galvanized urn. He gulped large and swished the liquid 'round his mouth 'fore swallow'n' it and the jerky.

"That's some good jerky. It's not spiced. I prefer it that way. All these guys are always peppering and hot saucing their jerky and then pretending like they like it when their foreheads sweat. Jerky was made for sustenance. It's easy to transport and it keeps a long time. On top of that, it's protein. So what else could a traveler ask for? You see all that extra spice is a mockery of jerky's original purpose."

He tore 'nother chunk and aggressive masticated. He walked over to the drop leaf and plopped a seat. Motion'n' me to plop 'cross, he tilted the jerky to me. I stilled.

"What's the matter? You don't eat breakfast?"

As Tumult ground the jerky and swished the water, I were able to calm 'nough to figure more 'bout what danger I might be in and how to wash it. If worse were worse, I could pitch a chair at his nog and probably easy out-sprint him. I'd scamp to the river and submerse so as the current could float me toward Pittsburgh and civilization. I didn't desire to 'turn there, but if it were 'tween that and porno-perv'n', the opt were crystal.

Tumult had forlorned the gun on the porch which meant that he either didn't eye me threat, or he were without care. I wondered if I could secure the gun, arm it and utilize it to buckshot this perv over a hill. This seemed unlikely 'cause even if I could secure the gun, the ammo I had were in the army foot and it'd be difficult to procure. The river escape 'peared my ace option. As I thought 'dditional 'bout it, Tumult posted, stowed the jerky in the army foot, sat the tin cup on the counter and faced me.

"What happened to the knife?"

"What knife?"

"The knife that was sitting here on the counter. It's gone. What happened to it?

"How should I know? Maybe it grew legs and walked 'way 'cause it don't like you."

Tumult flashed and wheezed.

"You're funny, Goldilocks. A genuine comedy act. But missing knives are dangerous knives. We don't want anyone getting hurt now do we?"

"Like I said, I don't know what you're talk'n' 'bout."

"I've got my eye on you Goldilocks. No sassy girl is gonna cut me, so I'd put away whatever idea you got about that in that pretty little head of yours. Lift your arms."

"Lift my arms?"

"Lift them. You appear to not have much on so if there's a knife in your waistband, when you lift your arms, I'll see it."

"I ain't got no knife."

"Then do me a favor and lift your arms."

I reached. The jersey rose and my naked mid exposed. Satisfied that I weren't knifed, Tumult 'llowed me to lower.

"Well there was a knife and I know you stashed it, but least you're smart enough not to carry it on your person."

"I'm smarter than I get credit for and so's my father but 'side smarts, he's also got a Winchester."

"Had a Winchester."

"What?"

"Your father doesn't have anything anymore, so it stands to reason that he had a Winchester not that he has a Winchester."

"You can 'splain that to him right 'fore he pumps a hunk of lead thru your face."

Tumult wheeze-flashed 'gain and some spittle dripped in his beard.

"What you say we head back to the porch? It's a beautiful morning."

Altho I would forfeit the chair as a potential weapon, I would gain a superior position to sprint the river from the porch so I followed. My legs momentarily rubbered and I RQD to brace the drop leaf.

"See what happens when you don't eat? Nope, breakfast is the most important meal of the day and you young girls are always wanting to be so skinny that you skip it and then you get too weak to get through the day."

Strength regained to my legs, and I followed Tumult out. He hand-rolled a cigarette from a pouch in his shirt pocket and Zippoed it. He drew a deep inhale and then coughed as he exhaled.

"I ought to quit these things some day, just not today."

He re-coughed as he wheeze-flashed.

My father always pontificated that a bandage were best removed quick so I marked the point there and then.

"What're you do'n' here? This is my father's cabin and you're trespass'n'."

"Was your father's cabin."

"What?"

"Your verb tenses are all screwed up. You keep talking like your father's around. This was his cabin, and he had a Winchester. It's not is and has."

Tumult dragged off the cigarette and exhaled. He clamped the 'mainder in the corner of his mouth and palmed both hands on the split rail. Eye'n' into the trees he re-spilled.

"Nope, this is not your father's cabin."

"Not my father's cabin? My father bought this place like ten years ago, and I watched him repair and rehab it. I've been here a hundred times. This is definitely my father's cabin."

"Goldilocks, you don't belong here. You're out of place."

I palmed both my hands on the split rail and now, like Tumult, I eyed out into the Allegheny trees. Aside from several squirrels scamper'n' 'cross branches, there were hundreds of trees tall post'n' and commence'n' to leaf. Among them were the fallen and decay'n' ones—the ones that either rotted or were diseased or storm-toppled. These were most the one's my father would utilize whenever we RQD wood resupply. Erect and timbered trees comped the landscape 'round the cabin and I suppose comped nearly any wooded landscape. I noticed one hickory that obviously had toppled within the year. It leaned 'gainst a high oak. It were uprooted, and I figured it must have storm-toppled or succumbed to ice weight. It were unfathomable that a tree, any healthy tree, could just be toppled and uprooted. Trees are so substantial and deep grappled in the ground. I 'membered back to the time when I eyed my father root up an old stump from the yard. After he learnt me to count rings and to identify the species, he set to maul'n' and spade'n' and pickax'n'. It RQD several sevens of 'tack'n' roots 'fore he had loosed the stump 'nough for the neighbor to tractor-pull it out with a chain. It took a tractor and sevens of manual to remove one stump from a yard yet here were an entire healthy tree—fact a tree that 'mained in leaf and 'parent unaware that it were kicked —uprooted by nature herself. It fathomed difficult like it were also fathom'n' difficult to figure what Tumult were deal'n'.

Tumult flicked the cigarette into the duff. He turned and then folded to rummage something in his tattered duffle which he had deposited on the porch floor. While he did this, I eyed his shotgun. He had been care to remain it broke and the barrel point'n' off the side. From the duffle he fisted two buckshot shells, walked to the gun, slipped one shell into the butt end of each of the two barrels and clicked the gun straight. He returned to the split rail, raised the gun and discharged a round into the tree tops. The report were top decibel and echo. The shot were reckless and gratuitous. My father treated firearms sacred and 'ways palmed them with great care and reverence. To simply fire a shot—even mere eight-shot—random in the tree tops were foolish and an ace way to cause unintended consequences—my father would creed it were play'n' with fire.

"You're confused. You don't even know who you are. Paul Joseph... ha. You're lost and you think this is a safe place to be, but you're so wrong you think you're right."

Tumult discharged the second barrel randomly into the tree tops and 'gain the boom top decibelled and echoed and disrupted the AM peacefulness.

My legs rubbered and commenced to weaken. I tightened my grip on the split rail. The split rail felt safe and grasp'n' it were comfort. My father had constructed this split rail 'round the porch when I were a tyke. I had pedaled my bike over the edge think'n' I were Evel Knievel. I weren't, and I landed up nearly cleave'n' my skull. It were a sixty drive to the hospital where I were diagnosed with my first concuss. I'd suffer two more rock'n' soccer and knowed that I had only one more remain'n' 'fore the doc would rec I stop ball'n'. My gaze turned to Tumult and my knees unsteadied. I lowered myself to the porch floor so as not to face.

"I am Paul Joseph. I know that. I ain't a girl and this is my father's cabin. I know a lot of things. Like I know my father never mentioned nothing 'bout some wack named Tumult fire'n' buckshot random."

Eye'n' up at Tumult had weakened the strength my words might have hit and now I simply sounded childish and vulnerable.

Tumult finger-raked his long beard.

"No, your father could not have mentioned me."

My head spun. Who was this smelly, dirty, vagabond?

"What do you mean *couldn't*?"

I were Heinz 57 but frustrated too. Tears sated the corners of my eyes and one streak trickled the side of my face. I fought the tears, but Tumult noticed.

"How can you know where you are when you don't even know what you are?"

Tears were now free stream'n' my face.

"Are you a boy or a girl, Paul Joseph?"

"I'm a boy. I've always been a boy."

I pronounced loud and definitive, but I remained cry. Tumult reached a paisley kerchief from his pocket. He handed it. It were surprise'n'ly clean and fresh. I wiped the tears from my cheeks and forced myself to post even tho my legs 'mained half rubber.

"If you're a boy, then it looks like you've got a problem. Nature seems to be arguing the contrary."

My knees gave, and I faced like a broadside doe. When I woke it were dusk, and I were atop the bed. The bed were made, and I remained dressed. My shoes were AWOL and my foot were freshly bandaged. A tin of water set 'side on the night table. I sat up and palmed if the filet knife 'mained under the mattress—it did. I sipped from the tin. The water were cool and metallic.

Tumult had fired the hearth and was plopped in a wooden chair. His gray feet were near the flames. He eyed fresh showered and clean and had switched to dark blue denim jeans and a western shirt with snaps. The red paisley kerchief he had nurtured me were now secured 'round his head. Burn'n' wood and vegetable soup misted the cabin. 'parently while I were crashed, Tumult had sat the dutch oven on the stove to heat soup from the army foot. He had even sat the drop leaf with two mess kits that he had broken open and arranged to mimic manners tableware. When he awared I were woke and gulp'n' water. He questioned if I strengthen up to sit'n' table or if I RQD to grub in bed. I slid out of the bed, checked my strength-balance 'fore release'n' the foot, and walked to the drop leaf. I awared Tumult's gun lean'n' in the corner point'n' at the ceil'n'.

Tumult hefted the dutch oven to the drop leaf and sat it in the middle. I ladled soup in a bowl and remained the ladle in the pot for Tumult to do the same. The soup were warm and tasty. I hadn't grubbed all day and it seemed to aid me regain composure. I figured I'd slurp a bit more and then I could flip the remains of the dutch on Tumult's lap and sprint if fish 'rose

"You took quite a spill out there this morning. Does that happen to you often?"

I silenced and slurped the soup.

"So is this how it's gonna be? No thanks for the nurturing. You're lucky I'm a kind soul. There are some people in this world who might take advantage when they walk in on Goldilocks sleeping naked in an isolated cabin. Yep, you're lucky you got me instead."

I silently slurped. Tumult remained silent as well. It were crystal that he were now 'tempt'n' to out time me and force me to dig up his arrival mystery. As he slurped broth from a large spoon, he eyed at me till I felt I RQD to sound.

"Why're you here?"

I faced Tumult and bent the corners of my mouth down to hombre. Tumult swallowed broth, hand-towel-dabbed his chin and flashed.

"Where's the filet knife?"

Tumult winked and play-pointed the spoon at me. My hand trembled as I rested my spoon in the bowl that were 'fore me.

"The filet knife?"

Still flashed, Tumult sucked another slurp from his spoon. He swallowed, sat the utensil and flattened both his hands on the drop leaf.

"It was over there on the counter this morning when I first came in and now it's gone. The way I figure it is you either stashed it to protect yourself or a raccoon stole it."

He face-eyed me.

"I ain't seen no raccoons here lately. You?"

I lowered down at carrot and green bean bits afloat among the peas. Tumult picked up his soup bowl and drank the 'mainder. He sat the empty bowl down.

"Murderers don't usually tend to the sick and break bread with them. If I was gonna kill you, don't you think I would have done it by now?"

He posted and started red'n' the drop leaf as natural as if he were a maid.

"I understand that you're afraid. You think you don't know me and that you belong here and that I don't. You're thinking about this dude with a shotgun who all the sudden is at the foot of your bed. Look, I get it, but your problem is you don't know jack. You don't know if I'm to be trusted. You don't know if your mother is to be trusted. If Father Antonio is to be trusted. Hell, you don't even know if your body is to be trusted. And instead of trying to figure out these things, all you can focus on is why I'm here. Well, let's get back to the real question, why are you here?"

"I know why I'm here."

I announced and spoon-slammed the drop leaf. The bowl quacked and nearly upset.

Tumult picked up the dutch oven with two towels. He hefted it to the stove top and lidded it. He turned and eyed me.

"Oh, do tell. This oughta be good."

I were fatigue of wheel spin'n' with Tumult, and I 'tempted calm 'cause Heinz 57 were push'n' the needle to eleven. My father dealt what he labeled a short fuse, and I had eyed him blow often times over the years. He spit vitriol at referees and coaches. He cursed at drivers. He even serious pitched at my mother every few when there were no one else for him to berate. He typically didn't castigate at me, but he were full Heinz 57 motor'n' me to the hospital after the daredevil off the porch. I had a genetic short fuse, and, over years, I'd popped in my share of playground squabbles and slams. My rep were chippy on the pitch, and I topped in yellows. My coach marked it were trouble and that I RQD to work it. He creeded there were a difference 'tween aggressive and dirty and I stood one foot in both camps.

Tumult respilled the question.

"Why are you here?"

"Why should I tell you? I don't even know who you are. This is my father's cabin. I have a right to be here. You're the trespasser."

"A trespasser? You mean like a sinner? Do you think I'm a sinner?"

"I don't know what you are."

"What or who I am is not important. Life is about figuring out who you are, not who others are."

I flustered and confused and opted to switch the subject.

"How'd you get clean?"

"There's a camp shower out back. It fills with rain water and the sun warms it. It's quite nice. I'm surprised you didn't know about it. I mean with you claiming this is your father's cabin and all."

I had been trail'n' the woods 'round the cabin ever since my father 'quired it. There weren't no camp shower that I knowed of.

"Even us old grizzly types need to wash down once or twice a year."

Tumult flashed.

"Are you gonna hurt me?"

"Hurt you? You mean like punch you or shoot you or something like that? God no. What kind of maniac do you take me for?"

"Then why are you here?"

"You invited me."

"I invited you?"

"Of course you did. When we are lost, we often send distress signals to the world."

"Why do you keep say'n' that I'm lost? I know where I am."

"Do you?"

Here we were redux in circle. Tumult simply answered with questions and nothing resolved.

"How long you gonna be here?"

"Not much longer I'm afraid. I'll have to be moving on in the morning."

"So you came 'cause I invited you. You've told me I'm lost and confused. You fired a gun into the tree. You hauled me from the porch to the bed and cooked me soup. You washed in a shower that I didn't know was there, and now you say you're leave'n' on in the AM. If I was send'n' out some distress call, I'd say you have a strange way of answer'n'."

"I didn't come to rescue you. We must rescue ourselves."

"If you can't rescue me, then why'd you show up at all?"

"To remind you that you need rescued—that you're not doing so well. You need to figure some stuff out and hiding in your dead father's cabin isn't the answer. I can at least tell you that."

"But how do you even know me?"

"That's funny. Maybe you should ask how *you* know *me*?"

Tumult tossed a log on the fire 'fore reposition'n' the table chair to face the hearth. He plopped and leg-stretched-out-straight cross'n' one atop the other. He intertwined fingers 'cross his stomach and exhaled. I carefully posted and spun the chair to also hearth face. I plopped so I could eye Tumult's face.

"Why do you answer my questions with questions?"

"Do I?"

Tumult wry-flashed.

Tumult had been 'round for sixties now and so far violence free. Fact not even a hint of violence-threat. Altho he were definite stranger, the longer I were 'round him the more he were comfort and normal—like a book or movie that 'minds you of 'nother book or movie. You know it's not the same, but it feels familiar.

"It's under the mattress."

"Under the mattress?"

"The knife, the filet knife. When you first got here I stashed it under the mattress just in case."

"Were you planning on stabbing me?"

"I guess I hadn't thought it thru, but yeah, I suppose, if it came to that."

"Have you ever hurt anyone before? I mean really hurt anyone? Shot them or stabbed them or beat them up in a serious way?"

In my playground tussles nothing were beyond blood noses. Fact is that probably the closest I ever came to potentially really hurt'n' someone was when I were in a middle school circle fight that the entire school witnessed but that dudded 'cause the principal broke it 'fore it really popped. Afterwards the kid and me 'came common and till I grew long hair, girl tits and a shrunken area, we even pitched for the same squad.

"It's hard to really hurt someone physically. You have to see the pain and you have to see the suffering and you have to bury your compassion under hatred and anger. Most people regret doing that kind of thing. I mean you got the random psychopaths and all, but mostly, people regret knowing what they did to someone else."

Tumult hand-rolled a cigarette and fished his Zippo out his pants. He exhaled smoke at the hearth.

"No, it's not easy to intentionally and willfully hurt someone. I'm guessing you never have and I'd advise you to avoid it if you can."

I lowered at the floor. I 'membered that deer I rifled with my father. When I rifled it it felt aces and I were satisfied that my father prouded, but later that PM I guilted rifle'n'. The deer weren't hit'n' nothing wrong, it were simply wild forage'n' and jive'n' its life and boom I rifled it. I ain't shot nothing since and altho I never revealed to my father why, I gradually lost my dead-eye marksmanship badge.

"There's lots I'd avoid if I had a choice, but it's like I don't have many choices these days."

"Don't go feeling sorry for yourself. That ain't gonna help."

I eyed over at Tumult as he pulled a final drag, exhaled and flicked the butt in the fire.

"Maybe we oughta call it a night. You've had a big day."

"Well, no offense, but I'm go'n' to be glad to see you go. Has anyone ever told you that you're 'noy'n'?"

I flashed.

"If nobody ever stirs the pot, how do we find out what's fallen to the bottom?"

'fore crash'n', Tumult and me red up the table and washed the dishes in the dry sink. I tossed the gray water 'mong the trees. Tumult unrolled a blanket on the floor in front of the fire, reclined and produced a whiskey flask. As I back pulled the covers, Tumult questioned if I wanted a hit. I shook my head.

We each settled—Tumult on the floor and me in the bed. Then Tumult commenced more questions.

"Tell me about your father."

"My father? Well, to open he's dead. He died of cancer 'bout six months ago?"

"Your father's dead?"

"Yes."

"Are you sure?"

"Am I sure? I went to his funeral. I saw him in his coffin. I've seen his grave and helped my mother pick out the tombstone. Yes, I'm sure."

"Sounds like a lot of evidence, but it's difficult for a father to die. Maybe you should make sure he's really dead."

"He's really dead. Believe me, I'd know."

"How would you know?"

"'cause I live with it every day."

"Maybe you do, but maybe you just think he's dead and that's what you're living with? Are you certain he's dead?"

"Jesus, what's this all 'bout? It ain't like I want him to be dead, but he's certainly dead."

"When's the last time you visited his grave?"

"Are you hint'n' I need to visit his grave?"

"I'm saying that it is difficult for a father to die."

Tumult poked at the fire a bit, hit his flask and then yawned.

"I'm going to curl up here. Good night my son."

▲ ▼ ▲

I were woke the next AM by the screen door bang. A woman's voice graveled.

"Marty? Why are you still here? You were supposed to have been long gone by now."

I sat up and eyed a fire hydrant woman. She wore a head scarf and a heavy cape over a terracotta tunic. A canvas bag hanged off her shoulder, and her hard soled leather boots clapped with every step she took on the planks. I don't know why I questioned her call'n' Tumult Marty 'fore question'n' why she were there, but I did.

"Marty? His name's Tumult."

"Tumult? Is that what he told you? Marty, you oughta be ashamed of yourself."

"And who are you?"

The woman eyed at me.

"Who am I? I'm Tessie, of course."

Then she turned, walked over to Tumult who, wool blanket cocooned, were stretched in front of the hearth. He 'peared crashed. She popped Tumult with her canvas bag. Tumult grunt-stirred. The fire had burnt down to embers and the cabin were gray chill. No sun today would toast and bright the place. The air smelled ozone and 'proach'n' rain.

Still eye'n' at Tumult, Tessie scolded.

"Tumult, pfft!, you trying to scare people?"

Tumult rubbed sleep from his eyes and slowly sat up.

"Look Tess, I've got just as much a right to play this my way as you have to play it your way. Last time I checked you weren't in charge."

"Oh, I might not be in charge, but there is such a thing as protocol and protocol dictates that you're the ancient woodsmen, not the spirit of discord. You're here to bestow wisdom and offer guidance, not to scare Paul Joseph into hiding filet knives under his mattress."

I palmed under the mattress, but the knife were gone. Tessie turned to me and in a matter of fact manner nodded assurance as if indicate'n' she were here and I could cut worry.

"I put that ugly knife away before someone accidentally got hurt on account of it."

Tumult posted, slid on his shirt and started snap'n' it.

"A little fear, a little mystery... These are great motivators. Look at the pews on any given Sunday. Fear and mystery will fill a church faster than a water hose can fill a bucket."

Tessie removed her headscarf release'n' a surprise amount of auburn hair that thick-braid-tumbled below her middle back. At first I thought she were an antique hag, but sans the headscarf and with the long braid of auburn hair, she 'peared unageable.

"Maybe fear and mystery will bring people in, but it's wisdom and understanding that keeps them in their seats. Paul Joseph's already afraid and confused; he's already in the pew. You're not here to scare him further; your job is to help him figure it out."

"What do you think I've been doing? Goldilocks over there has a lot of cud to chew on on account of me and if you hadn't barged in here, I'd say the child might have even had a few more morsels to masticate before I finished a mug of coffee and moved on."

I stilled in bed. The blankets were warm and comfortable and, maybe I hallucinated it, but I 'member Tumult spread-'n' an extra blanket over the bed sometime in the PM. I didn't know how Tessie manipulated the filet knife from under the mattress, but with her in the room, I also didn't feel I RQD the knife. She were a knife and 'stead of me draw'n' the blade and confront'n' Tumult, she were drive'n' him gone.

"Now gather your things and get a move on. You've already kept Freida waiting. She was expecting you last night."

Tumult stoked the fire and laid a few dry logs 'cross the embers.

"Ha! Frieda doesn't know I'm late. She doesn't even know she's expecting me. So if you don't mind there Tess, I think I'll take a moment to gather myself before being rushed out the door like a bad odor."

Tessie walked toward me and plopped on the bed edge. She relaxed her shoulders. Tumult fed some small wood chunks to the stove and water-kettled the top. While the water were heat'n', he fingered thru his string hair and beard and gathered his duffle and his gun.

"You know Paul Joseph, I saw a box of shells in the foot locker. I was planning on inviting you to do some shooting this morning, that is before Tessie rained on our little parade. You see, it's good to target shoot. Not just to improve your aim, but more importantly to understand what's a target and what is not."

He winked at Tessie who half flashed.

The kettle whistled. Tumult spooned six heap-coffee-tablespoons in the hot water. He stirred it some and mug-poured the cowboy coffee. He palmed a mug to me and one to Tessie.

"Oh, so now you've got manners. Did you at least feed the child last night?"

"Yes, I fed the child. Geez! whatta you think I am, completely incompetent?"

Tessie sipped.

"Well, sometimes I wonder."

The three of us silently drank hot coffee and 'eared the start of rain. The drops quiet-thudded 'gainst the shake singles, ran the pitch and dripped off the roof edge. It would have to rain a while 'fore I could certain there were no leaks, but at least nothing sprang immediately and that made me slightly proud of my roof labor.

Tumult drained his coffee, dry-sink-sat his mug, and then reached into his pocket. He drew a gold coin and held it for me to eye.

"I always pay for my lodging, even if you ain't the innkeeper, Goldilocks."

He table sat the coin. Then he plucked his duffle and slung it 'cross his body. He walked over to the corner, palmed the shotgun, broke it, and let it nestle in his arm crook. 'fore he walked out the door, he eyed Tessie.

"Tessie, Goldilocks still thinks he knows where he is. You might want to start there. I think I planted the seed, but you're going to have to water it."

"Don't you worry Marty, I'll take it from here."

Tessie flashed at me.

Tumult opened the door, walked 'cross the porch and melted into the dreary. A strange loss-feel tingled. Tumult certainly hadn't been a great companion, but he did grub me and tend the fire and he even blanketed me with an extra. Altho he frustrated me with paradox and contra, in the short he were in the cabin, he had 'come familiar and somehow seemed like he belonged.

"Where is he go'n'?"

"His vocation is that of a wanderer. Like all of us, he is not fated to stay anywhere for very long."

"Does that mean you're not stay'n' very long either?"

"Most things are out of our control, Paul Joseph."

"Out of our control?"

Tessie posted and walked to the hearth.

"How about you get out of bed, and we go for a walk?"

"It's rain'n'."

"Rain is necessary. Some people spend their whole lives under shelter. You can't grow under a shelter. You simply dry up and wither away."

I climbed out of bed and tested strength. My feet felt solid and my coordination normal. Tessie questioned 'bout the black marker circles. I learnt her 'bout parts of my numb body and that I had circle-drawn to science if the numbness were progress'n' and to remind me to injury-check these areas carefully.

"That makes sense. You did step on that nail without realizing it."

"How do you know that?"

"Paul Joseph, why wouldn't I know that?"

I commenced wonder'n' where Tessie had stashed the filet knife.

"Come on now, get your shoes on. The rain's not going to last all day and if we don't get started, we're likely to miss it."

"Miss what?"

"You ask a lot of questions, Paul Joseph. Other people can't answer questions for us. You need to learn that."

While I shoed, Tessie knotted the scarf over her head carefully trap'n' her long hair. She reached for my hand. Her grip were soft and warm and, palmed, we stepped off the porch and into the rain. At first the drops were cold and unpleasant, but as we walked and my clothes wetted, I stopped notice'n' individual drops. I 'membered when my father hauled me to Canada, and we lake-swam during a storm. I had wanted to retreat out of the water, but my father pontificated we were already wet so why retreat? It hadn't 'curred to me till he had lessoned that that I were submerged in water while 'tempt'n' to shelter from the storm.

Tessie led the path to the Allegheny. It were a solid quarter mile trek and by the time we hit, my long hair stringed and heavied and my jersey girl-tit-clung. I self-consciousd 'bout that, but at least I were with Tessie and not Tumult.

My father and I had angled this river area often, and we had an aluminum canoe tree-chained. I don't know why it were chained. The canoe, like the shake roof, leaked like a trucker hat. When we initially acquired it, the leaks were pinhole serviceable but over stretch the canoe opened to water so fast that sans continue bail'n', it were basically of no use. Tessie eyed the canoe and motioned for me to plop on a timbered tree next to her.

"Do you know where the key is to unlock that chain?"

"My father always had the key. I ain't certain what's 'come of it, but it don't matter, that old canoe barely floats."

"Well, that's too bad. We could have used it. In fact maybe we still can. Otherwise, we'll have to find another way."

"'nother way to do what?"

"There you go again with the questions."

"You're confuse'n' me. Tumult did the same thing."

"Neither one of us is confusing you, Paul Joseph. You are confusing yourself."

"That's just it. Right there. If I ask what you mean by that, you'll just say I ask too many questions, but I don't understand what you mean and I certainly don't understand what Tumult meant by a lot of the stuff he said."

"Let's start there. Tell me something you remember Tumult saying to you."

"Why should I?"

"Why not?"

"'cause no one invited you here and no one invited Tumult here neither. I'm just mind'n' my business and then you two show up cause'n' trouble."

"Causing trouble? No one invited us? Oh dear, Tumult was right. You are confused."

"The only thing I'm confused 'bout is why I'm dumb stupid 'nough to be out here in the rain with a stranger who took my knife."

"You don't wanna be here?"

"Where's my knife?"

"Your knife? I thought you told Marty that this was your father's cabin?"

"It is my father's cabin."

"Then isn't it your father's knife? Stands to reason, doesn't it?"

"No it don't and irregardless of who the knife belongs to, where'd you stash it?"

"Now Paul Joseph, we don't need to play with knives. At least not right now. We have lots of work to do and the first task is for you to learn that I'm on your side."

"You take the knife that I had to protect me and then you want me to believe that you're on my side?"

"If I weren't on your side, don't you think I would have taken the knife and done something violent with it?"

Tessie flash-laughed.

"Imagine that, me slicing up some innocent child. Now come on, do I look like a person who'd do something like that?"

"What does a person who'd do something like that look like?

"Beats me, but they don't look like me."

"Then why'd you take the knife?"

"To protect you, of course."

"That don't make no sense. I'm less protected without the knife."

"Maybe less protected by outside threats, but certainly more protected from yourself."

I were cook'n' ¾s Heinz 57. I posted and dent kicked the canoe. The toe-kick crushed my foot and the pain mud-planted me.

"I thought you played soccer."

"I do."

"Why'd a soccer player kick a canoe with his toes? Don't they teach you how to kick?"

"I weren't soccer kick'n'."

"What were you doing?"

"I were frustrated and I ain't gonna kick you, so I kicked the canoe."

"Imagine what you would have done with the knife. Now get out of the mud and sit back here with me. We need to talk."

Mud swished 'tween my fingers when I aided my post. I plopped the timbered tree wet and dirty.

"What's one thing Marty said to you?"

I eyed the gray sky and 'llowed the rain to water.

"He said that I weren't at my father's cabin, that I don't know where I am."

"What do you make of that?"

"It's crazy talk, that's what I make of that. I've been here with my father many times. This certainly is my father's cabin."

"Try this. Let's just say that maybe you're wrong. Just try it on. What if you're wrong?"

"If I'm wrong, then I really am lost 'cause that place sure seems like my father's cabin."

Tessie eyed at me.

"Certainty should always be suspect."

'fore I could question mean'n', Tessie fingered up and indicated I should cogitate 'bout it some. I ground-lowered my eyes, and I cogitated 'bout what I were certain of—'bout what were facts. Even tho Tumult tossed contra, my father fact certain were dead. I fact certain were at his cabin and I fact certain were change'n' into a girl; yet, I knowed, like Tumult, that Tessie would push 'gainst the obvious facts. What I didn't know was who Tessie were, who Tumult were, why they were at the cabin, and how they knowed 'bout me.

"Who are you 'gain?"

"I'm Tessie."

"How do you know so much 'bout me?"

"Why wouldn't I know about you?"

"'cause I don't know you and you don't know me?"

"That's what you think is true. Remember, certainty should always be suspect."

The rain dried and a chill-breeze goosebumped my damp body. I slightly shivered.

"I know I'm cold and wet."

"That's the first observation you've made that I agree with. Let me see what I have here. Tessie walked over to the canoe, flipped it and rummaged thru the supply tackle my father stowed under the shell. She produced a wool military blanket and shoulder-wrapped it 'round me. The blanket were itch and rough, but the warm and dry dealt aces. The goosebumps flattened but my legs rubbered and I were grateful I were plop on a timbered tree.

"Things are what they are. I don't understand any of this that you or that Tumult have been say'n'."

"The mind is not just the body and the brain, it's bigger than that. Think of the mind like the air. It is inside of us, but also inside of everyone else and yet, it is all around us as well. Only the dead, the mindless, stop inhaling and exhaling mind. If you open up to this, then your mind is not your mind, my mind is not my mind, and your father's mind was not his mind. We are all one mind. Our thoughts don't just impact us, they impact the plants, the trees, the animals and, perhaps most importantly, they impact other people."

I silenced and cogitated 'bout this for some. I scrunched the blanket tight 'round my body and smelt the earth-scent of fresh forest rain.

"I don't understand. I believe my thoughts make me act certain ways and my actions impact others, but I ain't never heard of what you're talk'n' 'bout."

"Ah, there is the revelation of your misunderstanding. I'm talking about all your thoughts, even the ones that don't inspire action, your dreams, your fantasies, your secret judgements, your feelings of love and lust. These impact everyone else. Those who are closest to us feel the impact greater, but like ripples on a pond, every boat is raised and lowered to some extent."

"Boats on a pond?"

"If you're angry at your mother and sit in your room for a while until you calm down and then go on without expressing the anger, you've still impacted your mother?"

"No I ain't."

"You don't think so? You don't even know what's happening to you and yet you still insist on clinging to your belief that you understand the world."

I pressured behind my eyes and frustration blurred my cogitate. Tears marbled down my face as if it were still rain'n'. I scrunched the blanket tight and core-hunched. Tessie shouldered me and I melted in and hard bawled for some while Tessie back-walked her fingers up and down. When I settled, Tessie released and eyed me directly in the eye.

"I've looked and looked and the total number of minds I've been able to discover is one."

"I don't understand. You're say'n' people somehow affect me based on their unacted on thoughts? That's not true?"

"These idle thoughts actually extend from our bodies like exhaled air and they affect not only others, but the universe, the reality we exist in. All reality is just our collective thoughts about it. If we all think in time and space, the universe will conform to time and space. The more we think in some other way, the more the reality of the universe will change."

"Why are you tell'n' me this?"

"Because life has a way of giving us what we need when we most need it."

"So I need to be sit'n' huddled under an old blanket by this canoe?"

"Are you sitting by a canoe?"

"Now you're back to sound'n' like Tumult."

"I suppose you're right. Sorry about that. Marty has a strange way of initiating imitation. Let's try again using a different approach."

"How can we try 'gain when I still don't get what you think we're 'tempt'n'?"

"Oh, I see. Yes... of course. Poor dear, you're confused, which is only normal. After all, confusion is the basic state of existence. We are born confused, and we die confused. Life is in many ways simply fooling ourselves into believing that we are no longer confused. But I suppose this too is confusing. Haha. That's a bit funny now isn't it?"

The rain returned and a low thunder rumble sounded in the distance. It weren't a cold rain, but plop'n' outside during a storm were certainly not something I practiced. I blanket-wiped my face to little effect and then chin-tucked into the base of my neck and folded my shoulders in to shelter. I felt the warm palm of Tessie touch my shoulder. When I eyed at her, she reached close and embraced me 'gain. She were dry and warm and, like a human shelter, she enveloped me. I sat in her embrace for sometime while the rain beat and 'gain I bawled. Maybe that's what Tessie wanted all along—hard bawl'n'. My tears were a mix of frustration and sorrow. I never desired life to forge this way—a kicked father, a wack body transform, isolated and embraced by a stranger. Yet, as I hard-bawled, I also commenced to know that were exactly what my life were supposed to be all along —that things were forge'n' exactly as they always were supposed to forge. My hard-bawl'n' started to settle and a calm slowly crept like a fresh blanket. I felt like several candles had been lit and the forest were a fantasy book. The rain subsided and Tessie's embrace slipped 'way.

"What's go'n' on? Why do I feel so calm now?"

"You are learning. You see, a turtle is a turtle even if it wants to be a frog. Eventually we learn that swimming upstream is laborious and futile. It takes constant effort and eventually the current will direct us whether we like it or not."

We silenced and eyed the Allegheny. The rain were now merely a drop here and there and every so often a ripple ring would 'pear on the glass surface of the river.

Tessie fished into her cloak. When her hand emerged, it were palm'n' a tarnished and tattered key.

"Let's see if this might just allow us to untether that leaky canoe?"

Of course it did and 'fore trudge'n' the canoe to the water's edge, Tessie produced a tin that eyed like it might house shoe polish. She unscrewed the top and revealed deep green paste that smelt strong of pine and oranges. She finger-gobbed and paste-smeared the canoe seams. It took a while to smear all the seams, but she labored methodically and without hurry.

"Let's see if this will help with those leaks."

I fatigued as I sat there eye'n' Tessie paste-smear the canoe seams, and I must have crashed off 'cause it RQD
Tessie's shoulder-palm to 'mind me that I were plop on a
damp timbered tree. Follow'n' Tessie's lead, we hefted the
canoe into the river and while Tessie stern-steadied, I manipulated up to the bow seat and settled. Tessie shoved off.
My father had left two oars bungeed under the thwarts. We
freed them and manipulated the canoe toward the middle of
the channel. The cool of the aluminum seat soon penetrated
my damp athletic pants and I body-shivered. The paste that
Tessie had seam-smeared 'peared to be solid as the belly
were not collect'n' water.

We paddled slow and indiscriminate. The current were
slight and the surface surprise glass 'sider'n' that we had just
experienced a heavy rain. I figured the run-off might still be
spill'n' into the river and thus we were experience'n' the calm
'fore the storm, but then I 'membered that my father stowed
the canoe in this particular spot 'cause it were near a subchannel of the actual river and that this particular sub channel were most always fair calm and still due to timbered
trees, large stones, and settled debris upstream. My father
lessoned they served a natural barrier that produced this little haven of gentle flow water. Tessie seemed to know all
'bout this as she controlled the canoe direction 'way from the
mouth to the main channel. Once we were a decent distance
from the bank, Tessie dropped the make-shift anchor which
somewhat stopped us from drift.

Me and my father had made the anchor one AM past
tense by pour'n' Quikrete into a large empty coffee can and
hold'n' an eye bolt in the middle of the thick mix till it set
'nough to hold the bolt on its own. Once the sludge were
hard, we eye-bolt-tethered a long yellow nylon rope and
there we had an anchor. My father commented that since it
didn't have no flukes it would be easy to haul it up when we
wanted, but that the trade were that it would slow the drift
but would not lock like a naval anchor. So with our new an-

chor in tow, we canoe-trekked, unchained it from the tree it were strapped to, stern-deck-secured the anchor and shoved out to science it. Once we floated to the subchannel middle, my father sank the anchor and 'llowed the cord to run the seven or eight feet to the bottom. We had feets of cord remain'n' and my father tied it off 'round his seat leave'n' slack. The anchor created 'nough drag that we most just slow circle turned 'round that center point. It were a sun day and my father bared his shirt off and 'lowed the warm to soak his skin.

My father's chest were hair and his pecs fair defined from years of pushups he repped out every AM. I were only seven or eight then and felt scrawny and weak and 'member cogitate'n' that future tense my body too would stone into the man body of my father. This memory reality-snapped me and a strange shame washed me.

"There's nothing to be ashamed of."

"There's nothing to be ashamed of?"

"That's correct."

"But..."

"There's nothing to be ashamed of. It's all about acceptance."

Tessie flashed and her worn old hands gripped the nylon rope and hoisted in the anchor.

"Let's paddle in, walk up to the cabin and change into some dry clothes."

We cabin-trekked in silence. My sneakers made muffled squishes as they pushed down into the damp leaves that covered the old river path. Like everything else 'bout the cabin, the path itself 'minded me of my father. When he claimed the cabin and built it habitable, there were no clear river path. He had to carve out the path with a chainsaw and a machete. The fallen trees that he sawed sections out of still lay on either side of the trail. Some were part decay and hollow but others were still solid and substantial. My father had sawed the sections into smaller sections and then split those for firewood which I had to cabin-lug a few logs at a time and stack 'tween two black locusts that stood near the porch. My father identified the trees as black locusts and pontificated that whoever originally pieced the cabin must have spared these two for a reason that is now long lost. The cabin were primarily white ash, sycamore and black locust and why these two relics were left stand'n' when they were so close to the construction is a mystery that will forever be unknown. The sycamore wood part of the cabin is what my father best loved. When he high-school-graduated, he promptly hitched to Florida where he romantically planned to live a beach bum and tourist-rent cabana chairs. He played that for close to three years and when I questioned why he hit back to Pennsylvania, he spilled that he missed sycamores. In south Florida near his rental, a developer were raise'n' a condo complex and one day three semi rigs loaded down with sycamore trees arrived. The developer planned on plant'n' them 'round the perimeter. To my father they were a 'minder of the forgot midwest. After that, his heart just weren't in Florida no more and when his lease upped, he drove an old Ford back to Pittsburgh and hunkered in my grandparent's basement. Eventually he locked my mother and they got married and that followed to me. In his head, I owed bank to the sycamore wood that helped hold that old cabin 'gether.

It RQD considerable time for the path to be clear and during that time, he had split and I had toted 'nough wood to make a solid wall 'tween those two black locust trees. The stack reached 'bove my head. Saw'n', split'n', and tote'n' the wood were serf work, and I resented be'n' the grunt whose dull labor it were to tote and stack. I desperately wanted to power the saw and at one point my father 'llowed me to run the spin'n' chain thru some of the scraggly branches. Sawed up, these branches produced inferior firewood that were too thin to split but, as my father creeded, would still burn. He held the saw with me as he posted behind and reached 'round. He learnt me how to squeeze the trigger to bring the saw to life. Neither of us bothered with ear plugs nor goggles and as the saw ripped thru the first few limbs, I squinted to avoid be'n' blinded with fly-debris. My ears rang from the engine roar, but the saw felt power and danger and since I had yet to gun-fire at that point, it were certainly the most potent device I had palmed. The saw ran thru the small limbs as if it were pass'n' thru tubes of water and the raw cut'n' capacity made me feel invincible—with this saw rear'n', I were safe from any foe. Who would dare to 'tack a man with a scream'n' chainsaw?

After slice'n' thru several brush limbs, the saw arm pinched and chucked the chain which startled me at first but which ultimately did no harm. My father kilt the motor and aided me pry the saw arm loose. 'fore he remounted the chain, he decided that since the arm were already loose, he would swap the chain with a new honed one. With the new chain mounted, he adjusted the tension, filled the chain oil and fuel, and got us back to work. That were the end of my chainsaw'n', and I turned to the menial log haul'n' and stack'n' serf. I thought 'bout that as Tessie and I meandered to the cabin in soggy clothes. The path had suffered little from neglect over the years and other than the 'cumulated damp duff, the trail were easy to trod and pleasant. Tessie walked front and had removed her headscarf. I noticed that her hair, like my mother had done to mine, were tightly braided and secure at the end with an intricate weave. Tessie's hair had flipped to ashen, but held thick and supple and 'gain I wondered how old she were. As we walked, the sun burned off the 'main'n' clouds and the sky brightened. It were mid-afternoon and the sun peppered thru the trees every once in a while catch'n' my eye. Since we were most amidst trees, there were little warmth provided by this new arrived sunshine and till we reached the cabin, there were no hope for our clothes to begin to dry. As we entered the clear'n' 'round the cabin, the sun's rays hit full and the warmth washed over us and helped alleviate the wet-clothes-chill.

We stepped onto the porch. Tessie turned and motioned for me to plop on the split log bench 'side the door.

"Go ahead and peel off those sneakers and socks and wait out here while I change. You might have grown breasts and long hair, but you certainly aren't a woman. I'll change in private and then step out and wait while you find something dry to put on."

I obeyed without objection. Tessie slipped out of sight into the cabin. I unlaced my sneakers and flipped my socks inside out yank'n' them off my feet. I began to wonder what Tessie meant by her comment that I weren't a woman. How did she know what had 'curred? Why weren't she fooled by my physical 'pearance? I had not spilled nothing 'bout any of the changes, yet somehow she seemed to intuitive 'bout my recent and unwanted transformation.

When Tessie 'turned, she were wear'n' a faded pair of loose blue jeans and an oversized flannel rolled at the sleeves. Her feet were bare and gray. She palmed thick wool socks and battered leather lace-up-boots.

"Your turn to change. You'll be surprised how good it feels to get out of wet clothes and into something fresh. Bring your wet stuff out here to dry in the sun after you change and grab my wet jeans and shirt as well."

I followed instructions, and, after root'n' thru the duffle, pulled out a cleanish pair of athletic pants and a long sleeve tee. The tee were a team tee that were presented when we won league last year. It had my last name on the back. As I slid it over my head and fished my arms thru, I pulled it down over my chest and ran my hands under my hair slide'n' it free from inside the shirt. I noticed that my girl tits were fair obvious defined just rest'n' bare under the fabric and that my nipples raised little bumps in the shirt. To face Tessie like this felt embarrass'n' and I briefly wished I had stowed the bra my mother had bought me so as to have something to cover me up a bit more.

I gathered the soggy clothes and toted them to the porch. Tessie had her socks and boots on by that time and reached for the wet clothes that I were hold'n'. She flung them over the rail to dry in the sun. Then she plopped on the step and motioned me to plop 'side her. I crossed my arms 'cross my chest.

"Do you know what an old-timey minstrel show is?"

"No."

"Well, sometime after the Civil War, some white people thought it was entertaining to paint their skin black and perform silly skits and songs on stage."

"Blackface?"

"Right."

I expected Tessie to continue, instead she raised her arms 'bove her head and stretched.

"I'm tired. Maybe a nap is in order."

"A nap?"

"Yes, a good old fashion nap and then maybe we can figure out what you've got in this cabin that we can make into a decent meal."

"A nap? What's go'n' on?"

"I'm tired and a nap would feel good. Nothing's going on."

"Just like that? Let's go take a nap?"

"Just like that."

"Why'd you just mention blackface?"

"Seems obvious."

"It ain't. Hey, by the way, where's the knife?"

"You don't need to worry about that. The knife is safe."

"Says you."

"Yes, says me. Now let's take a rest."

"Why are you here?"

"That's obvious, isn't it?"

"Blackface ain't obvious and neither is why you're here?"

"Do you have any money?"

"Money?"

"How do you plan on surviving without any money? You want to know why I'm here, but that's the least of your problems. Maybe you should recognize a blessing when you get one."

"I've got the gold coin Tumult gave me. That's got to be worth a bunch."

"That coin is not for spending. The man you call Tumult and even me for that matter, are not here to help you further your little stunt."

"Then why are you here?"

Tessie stood up and walked into the cabin. As I scampered to my feet to follow, my legs rubbered and I faced 'gainst the rough boards of the porch floor. Tessie either didn't notice or intentionally ignored it and as I bent up to a sit, the screen door banged shut. My legs felt numb and unresponsive. I sat there propped by my arms. I were scared and helpless and my first thought was to call out to Tessie, but I didn't. 'stead I lowered down to the porch floor and rolled onto my back. I didn't know what was flow'n', who Tessie was, why my legs were rubber, and why my body had sprouted girl tits and long hair. A few tears trickled my cheeks. Frustration overwhelmed. I must have bawled to crash and 'mained crashed for sometime 'cause when I opened my eyes, the sun were 'way and dusk were fade'n' to night. I rolled over and slow started to post. I were careful to science my legs and altho they seemed to be reliable, I 'mained cautious.

Inside the cabin, Tessie were stir'n' a large pot on the stove that smelled like some type of stew. There were several candles flamed 'round the cabin and the two ceil'n' suspended oil lamps were burn'n'. The cabin hit home and invite. I worked to the table and plopped.

"Welcome back to the land of the living."

Tessie flashed.

"I made a rabbit stew. You can have some now, but it'll be better if you let it simmer for a bit yet."

"You made stew? Rabbit stew?"

"Yep."

"I only have some canned soup, jerky and protein bars."

"Oh, don't you worry, Tessie knows how to survive in the woods."

Tessie hefted the galvanized pot from the stove top after towel wrap'n' the handle. She carefully poured steam water into tin mugs, sat the pot back on the stove, and toted the mugs to the table. She plopped one in front of me and sat the other on the tabletop in front of the chair where she plopped. The mugs smelled cinnamon and honey.

"I made us some tea."

"Was there tea here? I didn't know that."

"I always travel with a satchel of tea. One never knows when one might want a good cup of hot tea."

Cautiously, I mouth-lifted the mug and gently blew on the surface 'fore I sipped. I probably could count on one hand how many cups of tea I've downed in my life, but that tea tasted familiar—like an old shirt that has over the years taken on your body form or a soft worn blanket that you've cuddled under too many times to count—natural and correct.

"Well Paul Joseph, what are you going to do?"

"What am I gonna do?"

The question were direct and startle'n'.

"How'd you know my name?"

"Of course I know your name. Now, let's get to the brass tacks and focus. What are you going to do?"

I table-sat the warm mug and fingered thru my long hair.

"What can I do?"

"It seems like you have decided to do nothing."

"Nothing. I'm hide'n' in my father's cabin, and I've run 'way from home and my friends."

"This is not your father's cabin."

"Tumult said that too. It didn't make no sense when he said it and it don't make no more sense when you say it."

I tensed and were pop'n' ¾s Heinz 57.

"How can a dead person own something? It is basic Government 101. Maybe you should pay attention in your classes instead of texting with Jessica."

"How do you know 'bout Jessica? And how do you know my name?"

"Paul Joseph, why wouldn't I know these things?"

"What are you a ghost or something?"

"A ghost? No, I'm no ghost. This isn't some twisted version of a Dickens' tale but you probably don't know who Dickens is, do you?"

"Dickens?"

"Yes, the great 19th century English writer. Maybe you should take some time away from the pitch and expand your knowledge. Perhaps you might have even avoided this predicament that you find yourself in?

"Where's the knife?"

"You need to forget about the knife. We're talking about Dickens. Charles Dickens."

"You sound crazy. I don't care about some antique. How's that go'n' to stop me from turn'n' into a girl?"

"Turning into a girl? You're not turning into a girl."

"Then what are these?"

I pointed toward my chest.

"Paul Joseph, long hair and breasts don't make you a girl any more than black paint makes you black. Identity is not that simple."

"What does this make me then?"

"To start, it makes you a sad child with a dead father."

"Couldn't I be that without the long hair and the girl tits?"

I thought briefly 'bout the changes lower down.

"Besides, there have been other changes too."

"Paul Joseph, even if you started to menstruate, you still wouldn't be a girl. You're not changing into a girl."

"I'm not change'n' into a girl?"

"How could you? Changes like that are internal. Do you feel like a girl? Do you think like a girl? Do you have the perspective of a girl? Changing your body to match a perspective is one thing, but that's not what's going on here. Believe me, you're far from being female."

Altho this were reassurance, it slapped like a criticism. My competitive nature were triggered.

"What would you know 'bout it? When's the last time you woke up a boy?"

I hard-slapped the table. My face reddened, and I rose to my feet full Heinz 57. This were messed up and I wanted the knife and I were gonna 'quire it. But, my legs rubbered and I had to brace the table to stop from face'n'. In the process, I flipped my tea. The hot liquid splashed my lap as I plopped the chair.

"Finally."

Tessie flashed and from somewhere produced a small towel. She palmed it 'cross. I blotted the towel into my lap. Tessie reached for the mug and carried it to the stove where she refilled it and returned to the table with a fresh cup.

Still blot'n', I eyed at Tessie who posted 'side the table.

"What do you mean by finally?"

"You showed some real anger, and anger is a step in the right direction."

Tessie flashed and turned back toward the stove.

"Let's see how this stew is doing. I've got to scram soon and I sure would like to leave with a full belly. I have a long journey ahead of me."

"You're leave'n'?"

"Fish and company smell after three days. But you proba-bly don't know much about Ben Franklin either. Kids today and their soccer and phones."

Tessie pulled two old earthenware bowls from the open shelf 'bove the cook stove and ladled stew into each. She car-ried one over to where I plopped and then 'turned with the other which she sat in front of her chair. Out of habit, I bent my head and joined my hands.

"No praying here, Paul Joseph. Whatever god you might be talking to ain't currently doing you any favors. Maybe you should think about helping yourself."

"Help myself? What'd you think I've been do'n'?"

"You're trying to help your father and that is illogical since he's dead."

"I know my father is dead. Why do you keep say'n' it?"

"Do you know that? If you know this, what's up with the breasts and the hair and the stumbling?"

Tessie fisted the soup spoon and slurped stew.

"I'd compliment the cook, but that's me so I'll just enjoy the stew."

We silently ate with heads bowed over bowls till the bowls were near empty. Tessie laid down her spoon, picked up the bowl and drank off the remain'n' broth. She sat the bowl, cloth-wiped her mouth, and posted.

"I've never been a person who could go to bed with a dirty kitchen. Let's get this red up."

Tessie took the two bowls, the spoons, the mugs and the stew pot which were now most empty and loaded them into a galvanized vat.

"Carry these down to the river and rinse them out. Then fill the vat with water and bring it back here. We can boil the dishes while they are in the water and that should clean them well enough."

I did what Tessie asked but trek'n' the river and back proved a challenge. I faced twice trek'n' there, and I often rested on the return 'cause the water in the vat added weight. Eventually I did manage to return with most of the river water still in the vat.

I sat the vat on the porch, opened the screen door and stone propped it. I carried the vat into the cabin. It weren't till I hefted the vat to the stovetop that I realized Tessie were not in the cabin.

I didn't bother to search 'cause I knowed that she had skedaddled. I weren't exactly surprised that she were gone, instead I realized I knowed that she would be gone. Without Tessie the cabin weren't lonely as you might expect, but 'stead it felt natural, like it were supposed to feel. Tessie had been an intrusion, fact, more of an intrusion than Tumult. She turned out benign enough, but what she philoed were strange, and I realized that like Tumult had done, Tessie had spilled puzzle and paradox. I were, however, in no mood to

Sherlock. I RQD to figure out what were hit'n' and how to nip it in the bud.

The vat water on the stovetop eventually hit boil and water drops bounced out to sizzle 'way. I let the boil pop a while and 'eared the hiss splatters. I eyed 'round the now empty space and noticed that Tessie had placed the filet knife out on the counter by the dry sink. At least I had that back and that hit mid comfort. As a few more minutes passed, I gradually sensed aware that I were be'n' eyed.

▲ ▼ ▲

Sister Mary Ellen pontificated to the English class that girls rock fear much more often than dudes. She forced us to eye 'bout a weird perv named Arnold Friend who stalks up to this girl's trailer when her family's at a BBQ and he basically compulses her to ride 'way with him. The story terminals there, but we all knowed that he weren't just offer'n' to drive her to a burger joint for lunch. Sister Mary Ellen questioned the girls to jot out the last time they rocked fear and then she questioned the dudes likewise. When we showed, we learnt that most of the girls had rocked 'fraid at least once in the last day or two while the dudes most 'membered one isolated incident in the distant past. Sister Mary Ellen creeded that girls are, by nature, more vulnerable than dudes who often are stone and aggressive. A few of the girls balked, but it were crystal that Sister Mary Ellen had facts. When she questioned for volunteers to identify their frights, several girls spilled 'bout home alone, PM walk'n', and park'n' lots. I didn't spill my tale 'cause it involved Eric who were plopped two desks in front of me.

▲ ▼ ▲

Eric trapped raccoons and foxes in the woods by the Knepper farm and one day after soccer, he questioned if I wanted to hit with to spot traps. I didn't have nothing better, so I hit. As we motored out, Eric and I rated the girls we crushed and ripped lumps hold'n' the team down.

Eric steered down a gravel lane and slowed 'cause the lane were pitted with holes and highed with bumps. We passed over a cattle bridge and eventually parked in ankle high weeds. Eric kilt the engine and we posted out. He went to the trunk and inside were a locked hard-plastic black box. Eric unlocked it and revealed a 9mm pistol. He reasoned that sometimes a coon will snap trap but not be kicked and he'd have to between-the-eyes it. Whenever this 'curred he were care to pop it clean so as to salvage the pelt. Eric learnt me how the clip slid into the hollow handle and locked. I had some experience with my granddad's 12 gauge and an old 22 that were at the house, and of course my dad's 30-30 that I popped the buck with, but I had never palmed a handgun 'fore and didn't know how hard it aimed and the difficult of blast'n' anything more than a few yards out. On TV, lumps flew 'round corners and picked off each other sans effort and I'd assumed that were real. Eric were careful to close-range-blast coons 'cause it were easy to miss and either just graze the things or worse yet waste the pelts. I had no idea 'bout handguns and Eric agreed that lumps who have never palmed no handgun were pretty wrong 'bout how hard it is to trigger them.

With the gun ground-pointed, we hiked into the woods to spot traps. Eric led to each of the eight traps. They were all empty and two of them had been sprung and RQD reset. He were careful to re-bait each with a marshmallow. After we spotted the last trap, Eric eyed at me and flashed. When I questioned what were funny, he raised the gun and pointed it directly at me.

"Handguns aren't very accurate, but one never knows."

I didn't know if Eric were play'n' or if he were plan'n' to trigger. My impulse were sprint and that's what I did. I still wonder why I did not full sprint direct 'way. 'stead I shuffle-sprinted while all the time eye'n' the gun with my turned head. Hindsight, this were not efficient to put distance 'tween me and the gun. Maybe the desire to eye the danger were more important than the desire to distance 'way. I suppose it hits sense to always RQ to know where the threat is and if that threat is persistent, but it also hit sense to threat-minimize as much as possible and that would mean to distance 'way which shuffle'n' 'way while eye'n' the gun were not 'complish'n' efficiently.

When I were fifty yards or so 'way, Eric lowered the gun and flashed.

"I'm a terrible aim. I'm sure I wouldn't have hit you even if I did fire."

"You're sure you wouldn't 've hit me? What're you talk'n' 'bout? That was an asshole move."

As soon as I spit that last I regretted it. What if Eric turned offense and then really did 'tempt to trigger me? He still palmed the gun and I were vulnerable. Eric did not turn offense tho, 'stead he laughed it off.

"Yeah, I guess it was an asshole move, but you should've seen your face."

"My face?"

"Yeah, you looked like a deer in the headlights—totally scared shitless. Did you shit your pants?"

"What is this, some experiment?"

"I guess I just wanted to see what you'd do. Look, I'm sorry, I probably shouldn't have done that, but still, you have to admit it was sort of cool."

"It weren't cool. It was dangerous."

"Maybe, but no one got hurt. Let's head back. It's over now."

We silently walked back to the car. As we walked Heinz 57 morphed from fear. When we hit at the car, Eric ejected the clip, checked that there weren't no chamber-bullets, case-stowed everything and locked it. He latched the trunk. That's when I nose-fisted him solid. He faced the bumper on the way down. I dog-kicked his gut twice and then PK'd his balls. He rolled and gasped.

"Maybe that was an asshole move, but you should've seen your face."

I commenced hike'n' the long way home. I were 'bout a half mile in when Eric's car slowed 'side me. He rolled his window and invited me to ride. I climbed in. We didn't talk at all during the ride and after I exited the car, I never hung with Eric 'gain. I didn't seek no 'dditional revenge neither. I figured that we were even, but if he thought that kinda thing were rocks, he weren't the kinda dude I wanted to be 'round.

▲ ▼ ▲

Eric's gun aim'n' at me were the most fear I'd experienced. It dropped several months past and I still wonder if the fear intensified over other fears I might have had 'tween then and Sister Mary Ellen's activity, but I honestly couldn't conjure 'nother fear. That the girls could easily 'member recent fear struck me and made me wonder what my life would flow like if I rolled with a constant slight danger sense. Maybe this is what Tessie were pontificate'n' 'bout when she creeded that I weren't no girl. Maybe be'n' a girl were more than just pop'n' a non-boy body. Altho I thought 'bout this a while and even wondered what other experiences might differ 'tween dudes and girls, I soon 'membered that none of this mattered. Irregard of whether I actually were or weren't a girl, to most lumps who might eye at me, I were and would be treated like one. I'd already been porno-perved by a hospital freak and a gas station wack. I didn't creed that all dudes would be a porno-perv threat if I rejoined the world, but I rock how dudes think, and now on the receive'n', I know 'bout distortion.

▲ ▼ ▲

A wind gust blew a shutter 'gainst the window frame. The smack startled me and woke me out of my thoughts. I posted and, with two towels wrap'n' the vat handle, carefully heaved the vat of boil'n' water and sterilized dishes off the stove top and floor-sat it to cool. I stoked the stove-fire, tossed in a few wood chunks and latched the iron door that opened to the fire box. The cabin were comfort and the suspended oil lamps produced warm light. It weren't 'nough to tinker under, but it glowed a calm and quiet atmosphere. A wind gust slapped the loose shutter 'gain 'gainst the window frame. Like the first smack, this second one also startled me. When I went outside to secure the loose shutter, I found that the cast iron shutter dog were miss'n'. I briefly eyed 'round the porch, but due to the dark, I weren't locale'n' it. Not interested in 'tempt'n' to crash with a loose shutter 'casionally bang'n' the window frame, I drug the split-log bench over and end-turned it sos to pinch the shutter effectively 'gainst the cabin wall. I figured that that would suffice till AM when I could locale the shutter dog, figure why it detached, and fix it.

Altho secure'n' the shutter weren't exertion, I fatigued from the effort and, now that I knowed what to expect, were begin'n' to notice the rubber in my legs that 'lerted that I RQD to pull off my feet 'fore my legs uncled. I plopped the bed. Lie'n' there on my back, I realized the oil lamps were still lit and that I should extinguish them 'fore crash'n'. Not that it were all that dangerous, but it sensed a potential problem to shut-eye with suspended oil lamps flame'n'. But then it hit me, what could I rock 'bout the danger even if I were 'lert. If, like the shutter dog, the ceiling hook mysteriously failed, or a chain link give, the lamp would drop six feet to the wooden floor. The oil reservoir would seep and ignite 'cross and flame the old wood boards and 'fore I knowed it, the whole cabin, my hideout, would be ashes. The cabin were isolated, but a large fire would probably be noticed and the next thing I knowed there would be rubbernecks here—pervs and wacks other than Tessie and Tumult—real rubbernecks, who would RQ to know what I were rock'n': a teen girl torch'n' some lump's cabin. Sans ID or proof of anything, these rubbernecks would probably ring the heat and altho I'd protest, the heat wouldn't never creed that I weren't no girl and 'fore I knowed it, I'd be in the girls juvie reform. I RQD to extinguish those lamps, but my legs stayed rubber. A loud crash outside startled me and I realized that the split-log bench had fallen and the shutter were 'gain free to slap the window frame whenever a wind gust took. There must have been a weather system slide'n' in 'cause over the next sixty, the wind gusts slapped frequently and the shutter smacked the frame so often that it 'came to annoy more than to startle. Altho the cabin were solid and fairly sealed, I knowed that wind cranked drafts and I eyed the oil lamps that I feared might crash sway ever so slightly.

As I waited for my legs to 'turn, I eyed those lamps barely sway'n' and 'membered that, in fact, the last time I were ever here were shortly 'fore my father cancered. We had flowed the day hike'n' and fish'n' and labor'n' minor upkeep. We pan fried up smallmouth bass and grubbed them with rice and beans. When red'n' the mess, a storm slid in. 'fore the rain dropped in earnest, I scented the sweet pungent ozone. We learnt 'bout ozone in ninth grade. Mr. Franks, one of the few teachers at Sacred Heart who weren't no priest nor nun, once paraded us out right 'fore a storm and had us post in the lot and sniff. He learnt us that the smell were ozone and that ozone is storm-shoved down to the ground. I reck most of my group failed to smell it or just rocked the entire thing silly. Dudes started sniff'n' girls and lay'n' fart jokes, but I were engaged. I recognized that smell and had always rocked it sweet. So when Mr Franks learnt us 'bout what it were, I were interest. The ozone weren't the only clue of a storm slide'n'; the sky had quick-pitch darkened and the wind kicked and blew steady 'gainst the cabin front. My father popped out to secure the shutters. He tasked me to flame the oil lamps since the shut shutters would block natural light. When he returned, the wind were blow'n' so hard that he RQD to door-latch with force. He theorized we'd have to hunker and wait for the storm to slide. The storm weren't no tornado, but it were a mighty storm complete with boom

thunder claps and lightn'n' so intense that the flashes penetrated the shutters and flooded in. My father learnt me to
count 'tween lightn'n' and thunder to estimate how near the
storm center were from our locale. The cabin stood solid,
altho, like now, the oil lamps swayed slightly. When the
storm abated, daylight brightened for us to pop out and sur-
vey damage. The fish'n' poles were blown over and a tree size
branch were 'cross the front step. Otherwise, the cabin were
intact. My father specked we'd RQ to roof-inspect for damage, but that that could sit till the AM. I aided him drag'n'
the limb and then I retrieved the rods. As I plopped alone
that PM, I thought 'bout where those rods were presently. I
honestly didn't know. They weren't no longer at the cabin,
that were fact, and I couldn't 'member eye'n' them 'round
the garage neither. When my father cancered, things
changed and who knows, maybe someone borrowed the rods
or just took them or they got trashed. So much flipped over
those three years and there were so much commotion, a
crooked lump could've easily fingered a lot of stuff.

When the rubber left my legs, I carefully wound the wicks
into the burner till the flame dis'peared and then bed
plopped back. I crashed to the low rumble of far off thunder.

Confused 'bout how long I had crashed, a heavy door
knock'n' woke me. It rocked past sunrise, but it sensed early
like sixty or two sixties 'fore I would normally crank for
school. Manners dictated answer'n' the door, but I resisted.
'stead, I motionlessed in bed. The door pound'n' hammered
on and then the knocker uncled. Footstep sounds 'lerted that
the knocker were walk'n' 'cross the porch boards. I 'eared the
loose shutter creak as the knocker swung it, and I could eye a
dude-silhouette as the knocker window-peeped. The bed angled 'way from the window so I knowed it'd be rough to spot
me. The remains of the cabin presented still and calm. 'less a
wood-smoke hint from the cook stove embers odored,
there'd not be no path to know that the cabin were occupied.
The knocker window-tapped the pane as if the hammer-
whack at the door wouldn't have 'lerted no one. When the

tap'n' produced no signs of occupancy, the knocker walked back to the door and handle-jiggled it. I couldn't 'member if I had secured the door, but 'parently I had and the latch didn't release. I knowed this were it. Either the mystery knocker would certain of vacancy and door-kick, or he were merely a hike-thru and innocently eye'n' 'round. The jiggle halted, and I 'eared footsteps 'gain as the knocker took to the steps and ambled off. I stilled silent and sans motion for most of the AM and only posted when I absolutely couldn't hold my pee no longer. I were 'customed to porch-pee'n', but that rung danger now with the knocker maybe lurk'n'. The back door barred with a thick oak board that rested in iron slots secure-bolted to the logs. I lifted the board out, leaned it 'gainst the wall, swung in the door and ground-bounced. From back door to ground were several feet. My father never bothered to ramp no step. To him, the back door were just an emergency exit so there weren't no call to ramp nothing there. I peed without shame'n' on my shrunken area. Back inside, I pushed the door and reset the board 'cross it. It 'curred to me then that I RQD to skedaddle. Tumult and Tessie were bad 'nough, but this mystery knocker inkled especial danger, and I realized that I were vulnerable in an isolate cabin. Sensitive to make'n' smoke, I didn't rekindle a fire for cook'n' and 'stead grubbed a protein bar and water. I schemed on pack'n' the duffle, fire'n' the scooter, and head'n' out. While stuff'n' clean and soiled clothes together in the duffle, the knocker mounted the front porch and this time door-hammered hard. My legs rubbered, and I floor faced. As I lay there helpless, the pound'n' continued and then 'gain the latch jiggled. Then, as suddenly as he had hit, the knocker vanished. Whoever this were, they were 'parently not interested in forced entry. As soon as my legs would cooperate, I knowed I RQD to grip the duffle and mount the scooter and fly. In the mean, I 'tempted to formulate an escape in case the knocker were lurk'n' 'round or the scooter-fire blew my hide. Course, I didn't know where to go. I certainly weren't ready to land my mother and Father Antonio, don a plaid jumper and flow life at a girl school. I couldn't land Jessica. I hadn't hit her in forever and she hadn't eyed my body. 'sides, even if she did rock with it all, how would land'n' her aid? I couldn't develop no strat other than to flip the back door, push the scooter down the trail, kick it up and pray to speed 'nough to flee any porno-perv who might be woods-lurk'n'.

When my leg strength reached adequate, I lifted the back door bar, body-slung my duffle and ground-jumped. Almost immediately I 'eared a pig's grumble.

"Why are you hiding, sweetie?"

Startled, I cabin-spun back. The pig greasy-palm-clamped my arm and rotated me towards him.

"Run'n' 'way? That's no way to treat a visit'r. Ain't you got no manners?"

The pig posted a few inches higher than me and eyed total dirt. He wore a mountain beard and faded clothes. His muddy boots tramped unlaced and the steel toe of one exposed visible thru worn leather.

I silenced and shrugged his grease-palm off my arm. The pig eyed me.

"Whatta ya do'n' 'ere? This 'ere's private prop'ty. Anyone caught on 'nother person's prop'ty can be shot, ya know? It's Penn'vania law."

▲▼▲

When in a threat sitch, fight or flight. I 'membered the athlete creed: never be an observer. Be a star. It stranged to 'member that but I learnt it from a little league coach. My father took team stats, and we were vers'n' in the league championship. Directly 'fore we popped the field, the coach circled us and homilied us 'bout Willie Mays. I knowed the name as the name of some old time baseballer, but I didn't know nothing other than that. Like us, Mays were in a championship game but ancient back in the 50s. It came time for his side to hit in the bottom nine down 4-1. Seems they popped a run and then hit two runners on. So with the score 4-2, a dude named Thomson batted. First base were open and Mays swung on deck. The Dodgers deferred to intentional-base Thomson and decided to dice it. Thomson bopped a three run bomb. The coach pontificated that 'cause he wanted us to 'member something Mays coughed up years after. Mays preached that he were fear and nerves and relieved that the Dodgers pitched to Thomson. He didn't want to pressure-bat. After Thomson smashed the game open, Mays realized that if he were ever gonna star-shine, he'd RQ an attitude adjust. He RQD to be the one wank who absolutely wanted to pressure-bat—the wank brim'n' with confidence and swagger—that there ain't no stars sit'n' the bleachers. The coach preached us to 'member that you can either watch heroes or you can be a hero—one or the other. I realized that for a while now I were watch'n' and that I RQD to switch it up.

▲ ▼ ▲

"You're spot on 'bout one thing, this is private property, but you're the trespasser. I live here with my father, and he's due back any minute. Does that mean he gets to shoot you per Pennsylvania law?"

The pig took a step back and chin-lifted.

"Well, what do we 'ave 'ere? A sassy one I see."

"My father's got a pistol. Consider yourself warned."

"Consider meself warned?"

Brown globs of tobacco juice spilled out of the pig's mouth as he flashed. He back-hand-wiped his beard.

"How's 'bout ya ask me in and we set down and talk this thru? It sounds like one of us is in serious trouble."

The pig shoved me toward the door. I stumbled over the high threshold, scampered back to my feet and entered the cabin.

"Damn, it's a bit chilly in 'ere. Where's da fire?"

The pig eyed 'round. I positioned to the table far-side hop'n' that something between him and me would serve a block.

"How 'bout I light a fire and take the chill off? Ya got any grub to offer a visitor? Ya know I got to say for a trespasser you're not a very good host. Rustle us up some vittles while I rekindle this 'ere fire."

"Trespasser? You're the trespasser. If I were you I'd get out when I still could. My father's ex-Marines."

The pig ignored me and directed toward the hearth. He bent down to inspect what fire remained. I eyed for anything that I could utilize for protection. The thought of Eric gun point'n' me flashed 'cross my brain and of how I crumbled like a child and even once he lowered the gun, I still didn't lash till way later. I shamed that and considered it a Mays moment. I knowed I dangered now, but I weren't no bench warmer. This dirty pig weren't gonna dominate the sitch. Even if he senselessly whipped me which it seemed like he'd probably do, least at the end, I'd knowed I warriored.

I cabinet-stepped careful to grab the last two protein bars and two tins for water. The filet knife laid the counter and I pinched it in the waist of my athletics. Return'n' to the table, I table-tossed the bars and then started to water-fill the tins. When I spun the small water spigot, a slight tremor rippled my thigh. I knowed it were only a matter of time 'fore my legs rubbered. After water-fill'n' one tin, I quick table-backed and plopped a chair. I hit it 'fore my legs rubbered and fair certained the pig didn't know what were buzz'n'.

In the mean, the pig had transformed the few hearth embers to a decent fire and plopped 'cross from me.

"Now that's more like et. A little something for nourishment and some water. A pretty young lady and a warm fire. What else could a guy ask?"

"I ain't a girl."

"You ain't a girl?"

"No, I ain't."

"Sweetie, ya could have fooled me."

"I know what you think, but I'm a guy in a girl's body."

The pig eyed 'cross table. First he hair-eyed and then he lowered to the girl tits. The nipples bumped visible under the jersey fabric. I felt gawked and exposed.

The pig finger-raised like he were on to something.

"Oh, I see. Ya just look like a girl, but inside you're a boy. Is that it? I've heard of people like ya, but I ain't 'ever met one."

"People like me?"

"Yeah, people like ya."

"This is my father's cabin, and he'll be back here any minute and he's go'n' to be pretty pissed off when he discovers you here."

"Your father's cabin?"

"He went fish'n'. He's due back anytime now and he's armed."

"Anytime now and armed?"

"That's right."

Leg sensation returned, and I fingered the knife hilt.

"Your father da ex-marine?"

"Yeah"

The pig chuckled.

"I don't know whether your father were or weren't a Marine, but I know your father's stone cold dead."

The direct and assure of the pig's fact slapped me the same as if he had face-punched. I failed to poker the shock of not just this pig know'n' this, but also the 'minder of my sitch. I quick 'tempted to regain stoic and altho I suspected my blown ruse, I refused to bluff-concede.

"You're go'n' to wish my father were dead when he's done with you."

"Done with me?"

"How 'bout you get the hell out of here 'fore he gets back and maybe I won't tell him 'bout you?"

"Tell 'im 'bout me? Unless you's better at talkin' to dead people than me, I don't think you'll be sayin' nothin' to your father."

The pig floor-spit a tobacco wad, tore open the protein bar wrapper and savaged a chunk. He open-mouth chewed and guzzled water from the cup.

"Now that hits the ol' spot."

The pig table-left the rest of the uneaten bar next to the cup and posted to stretch. It 'peared a spot-time to blade-flash, but 'fore I could, the pig tossed off his soiled jacket and unbuttoned his shirt.

"Ya ever give anyone a wersh?"

The pig were fat and his pumpkin-belly fell over the waistband of his crusty jeans. His skin dulled ashen and splotched with coarse hair. With his shirt off, a rank skunk and sulfur odor air-stank.

"'ere's how it's gonna be my 'ittle girl-boy. You's 'ere alone, and I need a wersh. So we're go'n' to play a 'ittle game. Ya like games? Sure ya do. Here's how the game goes. You go over there to that there pot on the stove and put your hand alls the way in the water."

I stilled. The pig lunged.

"Do it!"

Startled, I complied. I hand-immersed in the water. The pig flashed like a deranged derelict.

"Good, now we knows the water ain't too hot. Now get yaself a towel or a rag or a sponge and bring it over 'ere 'long with that pot and wersh me off. I smell like someone farted into a dirty sock."

I ain't had no intention of wash'n' this pig, but I figured this were an op to close-draw and I maybe could damage something with the blade. The old pot had a bale handle, and I grasped it and hauled 'long with a dirty towel from the counter. As I 'proached, the pig's stench near gagged.

"That's a good gal. Now dampen that there towel and clean my chest and back. If ya do a good job, I might let you clean the rest of me, but you'll need a bigger towel, if ya gets my meanin'."

The pig gurgled and arm raised to fully expose his chest and back. I floor-sat the pale, knife-gripped and in one motion slid it out and plunged it in the side of the pig's chest. I were surprised how smooth the blade sunk. It were like stab'n' mud or wet clay. The pig doubled and groaned. I back-pulled the knife and thrust it a second. This time I shoulder-buried the blade deep. The pig swung at me but missed. I backdoor scrambled. 'fore I could release the lock bar which the pig had re-laid 'cross, his hand ankle-gripped and ground-yanked me. The ground-face caused me to drop the knife and the pig, now with a firm grasp on the bottom of my athletics, pulled. I wiggled and 'llowed the athletics to off-slip, and, waist-down naked, I regained my feet and un-barred the door. As I opened it, the pig body-slammed 'gainst me and the two of us cabin-toppled-out and ground-faced. The pig's girth crashed 'gainst me and hard-piled me into the duff. For what seemed several minutes, we faced dazed from the fall. Blood damped my jersey. My legs rub-bered, and I thought maybe I'd broken bone. The ground-skin chilled and the pig's fat pinned me 'gainst it. The pig strength-regained some and he hand-palmed the back of my head. He hard drove my face 'gainst the brown and broken leaves.

"You 'ittle son bitch. Ya shanked me."

He released my head and with both hands jammed 'gainst my back, he kneeled and straddled me. With an open palm, he slapped hard 'cross the back of my head and a low hum-ming noise sprung in my ears.

"Now why'd ya go and do something stupid like that? I thought we was havin' a nice time."

The pig's cold belt buckle slid 'cross my back-side as he unfastened.

"I guess ya like it a bit rougher, eh?"

As his hands lecher-pressed, I mustered all my strength and bucked into him. Maybe it were the two stab gashes or maybe I had nut-cracked him, but either, he side-toppled with a groan. Leg-feeling had returned with no broke bones. I gained foot'n' and jumped over the pig to the open back door and the blood-knife floor-laying. 'gain, the pig ankle-clutched and tripped me. I tumbled over the threshold which jammed in my gut like a Jimmy V rocket shot. While 'temp-t'n' to catch breath, I inched enough to finger the knife.

"Ya fuckin' son bitch."

The pig teetered to his feet.

"Fuckin' bastard."

As he dived me, I rolled and sunk the knife a third time. This time it lost in his gut as forward momentum rode the blade and my hand deep inside the gash. Blood sprung over my hand and arm and the pig deflated on top of me. I couldn't eye nothing, but it hit fact certain that the blade cleaned-thru and stuck out the pig's back. He convulsed. Blood and spit mouth-trickled out onto my forehead. The pig's dead weight ground-wedged me. My hand remained inside his blubber and everything stilled as the pig kicked. The wedge increased and, as the moment calmed, fatigue and fear overwhelmed. The sulfur and skunk stench gagged, and I coughed and bawled. I had expended whatever strength I had and then some defend'n' and now I couldn't free myself from this filthy glob. I certained my legs had rubbered in the final fight stage. I wedged-crushed down under this pig's fat long 'nough for his blood to start to cool and his body to stiff, yet I still were powerless to free my hand from inside his gut. Leg feel'n' came back, and my naked skin 'gainst the floor, blood sodden, iced. 'gain I fell into bawl as I imagined that this were terminal. I bawled on for some time and then I must have blanked 'cause the next thing I knowed I were gunshot-startled by a discharge boom.

"Let the child be."

When the kicked pig on top didn't budge, the man repeated his command only this time the actual sitch seemed to register. He bent over and, with some effort, flipped the fat body off me. My hand freed, but the knife 'mained in the dead pig's gut. I were drenched in gore and filth and naked below the waist. Feet-scramble'n', I palm-covered my shrunken area and stumbled toward the bed. I clutched the quilt and wrapped in it.

"And who the hell are you?"

I were fuel'n' an adrenaline burst and in no mood for 'dditional chaos.

"I'm the guy who just saved your ass. That's who I am."

The new stranger rifle-broke and positioned it over his arm.

"I saved my own ass. That pig were long gone 'fore you showed up. Whatta you want?"

"It's ok. Paul Joseph, you're in shock. Let's take a bit of time to calm down."

"Calm down? Fuck you. Who are you and why are you here?"

"You invited me."

"I didn't invite you. I ain't invited none of you and yet you all keep show'n' up."

"We all keep showing up? Who keeps showing up?"

"First there was some guy who said his name was Tumult but then Tessie said it were Marty and that pig over there and now you."

"So you've met Tessie and Marty have you? I hope they did not meet the same fate as your friend over there on the floor."

"That pig's not no friend."

"Paul Joseph, let's take a second and just breathe. You're really amped up right now. Can't say as I blame you, but it's time to calm down. I'm not here to hurt you."

"How do you know my name?"

"You invited me, remember, we already established this."

I eyed the blood-knife hilt in the pig's gut, but the stranger were 'tween it and me. I dove for it anyway. I quilt-tripped and faced. Still I army-crawled to the pig and pulled the knife. I sat bare on the floor and held the blade up full Heinz 57 and ready to lamb this perv too.

"Get out."

"Paul Joseph, let's just calm down here. I'm on your side."

"Get out."

"Listen Paul Joseph, I know Tessie and I know Marty and I know they didn't hurt you. How could I know all that? Besides, if I wanted to hurt you, why'd I roll that dead guy off you?"

I stilled but 'mained tense and ready.

"You're misperceiving. I don't know who that dead guy is. That's the honest truth. But I do know that Marty and Tessie and me are helpers, not troublemakers."

"Helpers?"

"Yes, helpers."

My legs rubbered and I dropped the knife in order to hand-tilt my torso upright. I were too fatigued tho and soon 'llowed the quilt to cushion my face. That, paired with the pig's head-knocks drifted me in and out, and it weren't till the lump water-poured me that I full gained my senses.

"Time to grow up, son. You've got quite a predicament on your hands and sitting around feeling sorry for yourself isn't going to help you now."

"I thought you were a helper?"

"I help people learn to help themselves. Now get yourself down to the river and cleaned up."

He tossed my duffle and a rag at me.

"When you get back here we can straighten this mess out."

I strength-tested as I utilized the chair to post. The wet quilt slipped off expose'n' my shrunken area. I left the quilt on the floor, grabbed the duffle and the rag, and stepped out the front toward the path to the Allegheny.

At the river, I briefly thought of canoe-jump'n' and river'n' 'way from this whole mess, but something sensed me that 'scape'n' down the river weren't the way out and 'stead I pulled off the ruined jersey, tossed it, and waded into the water to rinse the best I could. The water chilled, but, like ice on an injury, it soothed. I skin-rubbed and dunked under and fingered thru my hair and 'cross my face. I repeated the process several times and when I couldn't rock the water-chill no longer, I shore-waded and toweled 'fore rummage'n' thru the duffle for some reasonably clean athletic pants and a pullover. My mind calmed and altho I weren't look'n' forward to 'turn'n' to the mess-scene, I slid a pair of socks and athletic shoes and trekked the cabin.

The helper-man porch-sat as I neared. He pipe-puffed and his feet were propped on the split-rail. I silenced and plopped the porch swing. The swing-chains rattled. The new stranger sat quiet also and seemed to be thoroughly enjoy'n' the tobacco. The silence 'tween us were something new. When 'round others, my father motored loads and he learnt me to likewise, and altho I maintained silence for long as I could, I finally demanded to know the man's name.

"Name's Jessup."

"Jessup?"

"Yep."

"Ain't you gonna say anything else?"

"Like what?"

"Like explain'n' what you're do'n' here and how you know 'bout Marty and Tessie."

"I thought we already established that."

"We ain't 'stablished nothing. You showed up and rolled that pig off me and threw water on me and then told me to go get washed up."

"I believe I told you I was a helper."

"I don't know what that means?"

"We all need help every now and then. No man is an island."

"I don't need nothing from you."

Jessup flashed.

"Really?"

"I got here on my own and honestly I was do'n' just fine till Tumult or Marty or whatever his name is showed up. Then Tessie came waltz'n' in."

"So you think things would have ended the same with your recent visitor without Tessie and Marty's help?"

"Tessie and Marty's help?"

"Let's just say that dead guy in there was mighty danger-ous. Things could have gone quite a bit worse for you."

"If you're a helper, where were you when I was vers'n' 'gainst that pig?"

"I was exactly where I was supposed to be. We can be no other place."

"Bullshit. You were absent—awol. You were supposed to be here to help me and you weren't. You were a no-show and left me here to deal with this mess by myself."

"Like I said, I was exactly where I was supposed to be."

"When are you supposed to be leave'n'?"

I posted and 'gain the swing-chains rattled.

"Forget it. It don't matter. I was just leave'n' anyway. So hey, why don't you just stay and enjoy your pipe?"

My legs freshed and my adrenaline registered full. I pulled open the front door but then 'membered the lambed pig on the floor and opted 'gainst entry. I spun the steps. I'd go 'round the cabin, mount the scooter and motor the hell from this nightmare. Who needed this? I had 'nough to fret. I figured once I distanced 'tween me and the cabin, I'd strat out a new plan and hence from there. The secluded hideout, real facts, weren't secluded after all.

"Paul Joseph, no matter where you go, there you'll be."

"Fuck off Jessup if that really is you name."

I surprised me with the harsh and bold. Maybe lamb'n' that pig emboldened. Who'd know how lamb'n' a pig would alter a lump other than a lump who actually done it. Lam-bers ain't the common lumps I hang with, so I were trod'n' uncharted.

I climbed the scooter and kicked the starter. The motor didn't fire. I kicked 'gain and still nada. 'gain and nada. This indicated bad. The motor should fire. It had operated fine to haul me here, it rocked nonsense that it wouldn't spring now. Frustration slapped and I jumped the kicker with full weight and under-breath curse'n'. I final jumped to full force kick the pedal. I unbalanced and faced. The scooter wedged on top of me. For the second time that day, I were ground-pinned, but the scooter weighed less than the pig, and I squirmed from under it. I struggle-posted and righted the scooter onto its center stand. I eyed Jessup post'n' near palm-toss'n' a spark plug. He caught it in his mitt and then tossed it to me. Instinctively, I palmed it.

"I guess you'll be needing this if you're fixing to run off like a child."

"You took this from my scooter?"

"Just helping."

"Help'n'?"

"Let's go back to the porch and talk this thru. If after we talk you want to ride off somewhere I won't stop you, but at least hear me out first."

I posted and thought a minute. I weren't no mechanic, but I knowed 'nough to know a spark plug ain't something a lump can unscrew like a lightbulb. A socket were RQD, and it would RQ a socket to lock it back. This meant that Jessup had the RQD tool and altho he were pretend'n' that he were opt'n' me choice, a spark plug in hand with no tighten'n' tool were as useless as a ball pump sans needle. I were fair certain Jessup knowed that I knowed, but I opted to poker-cool and consented to the porch.

Jessup plopped 'gain with feet up and after pipe-fiddle'n', relit and exhaled three smoke rings that wafted apart. The air were fair calm and the day were sun and warm. Fact, it were a perfect spring day for a soccer scrim. The kind of day that rocks warmer than it would late in summer 'cause so many days previous had rocked cold and gray. I were born and raised in south-western Pennsylvania and altho I knowed that much of the world hit far more sun than my genome, gray and overcast normed for me and sun, when it hit, were always experienced with gratitude. This sun were different tho. The contrast 'tween the atmosphere and my predicament were off. The sun bathed me, but I chilled like full on shade. For the third time I porch-swing-plopped and the chains rattled. My feet back-n-forthed the swing. Jessup silenced 'gain, and I wondered 'bout the lambed pig in the cabin. Maybe I had been in shock and now it were dissipate 'cause what were courage and swagger were flip'n' to scare as I realized that I had actually lambed the pig. Lumps rolled jail for likewise. They rolled long-term jail for likewise. Would I be able to convince anyone that I self-defended? Me, a dude in a girl's body, a runaway, an 'cused drug user? And what 'bout the lambed pig? Who were he actually? Why did he hit here and what perv-porno would he have committed if I hadn't lambed him. That thought shuddered me and the memory of his cold belt buckle 'gainst my skin tremored thru me. My face tightened and tears dropped, but I had bawled 'nough. No matter what were in store, like Jessup creeded, it were time to face up and act. Course what exactly I could do were fog, but porch-plop'n' while Jessup lipped smoke rings weren't hit'n' me close to a solution.

"If you're a helper, then help. There's a dead dude in this cabin."

A slight breeze puffed and a cloud blanketed the sun.

"The dead guy's your problem, not mine."

"My problem? You've got to be kid'n'. You bust my scooter and tell me that I need to start face'n' my problems. Well the dead guy seems like a big problem to me and I'm face'n' it by ask'n' for your help."

"The dead guy certainly is your problem."

"Fuck you."

The chains rattled as I lurched to my feet. I opened the cabin door and eyed in. The place were a mess. The gory pig sprawled by the fire which were at present just a smolder ash pile. The chair were overturned and the wet and bloody quilt floored by the bed. The back door top hinge were bust and the door angle-hanged. My athletic pants were table-bunched where the pig had left them.

"You probably need that knife back."

"What?"

"The murder weapon. If I were you I'd retrieve the murder weapon. You don't want that around as evidence."

"So you think I murdered that pig?"

"Does it matter what I think? It matters what the police will think if they find a dead guy and a bloody knife on the floor."

I suddenly thirsted yet I couldn't bring myself to go in there for water. I turned and as if he 'ticipated my need, Jessup palmed a canteen.

"Here"

I unscrewed the lid and sucked a long draw. The water were cold and metal. I screwed the top back and reached the canteen to Jessup who motioned me to keep it.

"Thanks."

"Sit down, Paul Joseph. I know you want to act, and that's a good sign, but before you do, you need to figure out a few things."

I plopped the step with my back to Jessup and eyed the woods. The white tail of a rabbit bounced 'way and to my right two squirrels wrestled. I 'eared the peak and tut of a robin and the squawks from a vee formation of geese. With the sun and blue sky and the peace, I cogitated 'bout how idyllic everything would be if only I weren't plopped here in a girl's body and if only there weren't a lambed pig in the cabin.

"Would you be willing to walk through Hell to get to Heaven?"

"Walk thru Hell?"

"Walk through Hell."

"What? Who cares? I don't know, I guess it would depend on a few things."

"Like what?"

"Like if I knowed Heaven was real."

"Isn't walking through Hell evidence?"

"Maybe, but what is Heaven like? I mean I don't know nothing 'bout the place other than what I've learnt at church. What's this got to do with anything?"

"Just humor me."

"I've never met a person who actually went to Heaven and lived to tell 'bout it, but I did meet a person who kilt a guy who was attack'n' him and that person happens to be sit'n' right here and the guy he kilt is in this cabin right here."

"I think you're missing the point. I'm talking about Heaven and Hell, not your little problems. Don't you want to go to Heaven after you die?"

"Heaven? After I die? What if that pig's there? What if God has a twisted sense of humor and is let'n' that pig in right now.?"

"No one really knows who's in Heaven."

"Yeah, no one knows shit about that place so, what's the advantage of try'n' to get there? Why are we even talk'n' 'bout this? There's a dead guy in my father's cabin and I kilt him. Maybe we should be talk'n' 'bout that."

"We'll get to that, but first what's this you're asking? What's the advantage of Heaven? Certainly you know the advantage of Heaven. You've been Catholic your entire life and you even went to Catholic school, a place you're currently truant from if I'm not mistaken. So cut the crap and answer the question."

"Would I walk thru Hell to get to Heaven? That question?"

"Yes, that question."

"Fine. I'll play your stupid game. Let's see. Would I walk thru Hell to get to Heaven? Can I get to Heaven some other way?"

"I suppose it's possible, but what if those other ways were risky and this was a guarantee?"

"My dad never liked guarantees. He said they were sucker plays."

"Well suppose this one isn't a sucker play. It's real. You absolutely would get to Heaven if you simply walked through Hell."

"Absolute guarantee? Would I still be a girl? In Heaven?"

"Still be a girl? You're not a girl now."

"I feel like a girl."

"How do you know what it feels like to be a girl? You're a boy with breasts and long hair. That doesn't make you a girl. Come on, you already know this too."

"I know this? Do I? Just because Tessie said that doesn't mean I know it. How does Tessie know what it feels like to be me? Who made her the authority?"

"Nature made her and every other woman out there the authority. Don't you see? From the moment these women came into the world their bodies and souls were feminine and then the world treated them 'cordingly. They've learned from their first breath onward what it means to be female. You've had the complete opposite situation, so maybe you should climb down off your high horse and recognize that you don't know squat about what it's like to be a girl. Besides, like Tessie said, breasts and long hair don't define anyone anymore than facial hair and biceps define anyone. You've got to get past the external. Now answer the question."

"Why should I? It seems like a stupid question to me."

"What's stupid about it?"

"It's one of those philosophy questions that makes a hypothetical dilemma and the way you answer it is supposed to let you know something 'bout how ethical you are. Father Matthews used to ask these questions every Friday in Religion class. He thought it would start some deep conversation, but it's all bullshit."

"Why did you think that?"

"'cause I'm never gonna have to decide whether a train rails over one or five people and I'm never gonna have to choose 'tween save'n' a priceless paint'n' or a baby from a house fire."

"My question isn't like that."

"Yes it is."

"No, my question is about how you choose to live your life."

"Choose to live my life?"

"There are as many ways to live as there are grains of sand, but, regardless of what path you take, your life can be evaluated on a scale of suffering versus pleasure. How many of your choices were simply the easy way out?"

"I'd say hide'n' in a cabin with long hair and girl tits, not to mention there's other changes, might not be considered the easy way."

"Really? Looks pretty easy to me."

"Easy?"

"We run away and hide or we stand tall and endure."

"Run away? I didn't choose to wake up one morning like this. I didn't choose to be the boy whose dad died. My mother was gonna make me wear a dress and go to a girl school. Do you think agree'n' to that would be stand'n' tall?"

"Were living your life as a girl or running away your only two alternatives?"

"You make it sound so easy. It's not like I'm in Father Matthews' class and we are just mess'n' 'round. This situation is real, and I did what I needed to. Believe me, I wish it were different, but it ain't. I didn't ask for none of this."

"Are you sure? It seems like you decided not to walk through Hell to get to Heaven. You think there's a backdoor into Heaven and there's not."

"I don't understand none of that. This seems a lot more like Hell than play'n' soccer and hang'n' out with Jessica. There's a fuck'n' dead guy in my father's cabin and I kilt him."

"That's true, but it's still the easy way out of a situation that you didn't want to be in in the first place."

"An easy way out? You think live'n' out here 'lone in this cabin is the easy way? You think have'n' strangers who somehow know a lot 'bout me barge in here every other day is the easy way? You think that pig in the cabin is the easy way?"

"It certainly is easier than the alternative."

"The alternative? What's the alternative?"

"You tell me."

"Stay with my mother and go to Perpetual Sorrows? Live the rest of my life as a dude trapped in a girl body?"

"There are as many paths as there are grains of sand."

"Ok, so I run away 'gain, but this time go somewhere else. But I'd still be in a girl body."

"What else?"

"I don't know, kill myself."

"What else?"

"Let's see, rob a bank and use the money to get a doctor to make me a dude again."

"Why do you need a doctor for that?"

"Why do I need a doctor for that?"

"Yes."

"'cause I don't know how to operate on people and even if I did, I couldn't do surgery on myself 'gardless of how good a surgeon I were."

"You can't operate on yourself?"

"No, no one can."

"No one? If that's true, humanity's in trouble."

"What are you say'n'?"

"Think about it."

"You're say'n' I need to operate on myself?

"Maybe."

"You think the alternative to run'n' 'way or any other option is to figure out why this is happen'n' to me and then fix it. You think that is the path thru Hell that leads to Heaven."

Jessup's boots punched the wooden deck'n' as he posted. He bumped the spent tobacco out his pipe and shirt-pocketed the apparatus.

"Seems like it's time to do something about that dead guy in there. I'll go out back and get the ax."

Jessup walked off the porch. When he 'turned, the ax handle were over his shoulder and he palmed a whetstone. He step-plopped, pulled a rag from his pocket and half wrapped the whetstone. As if he did it everyday, he scraped the whetstone over the underside ax blade several strokes 'fore flip'n' the ax and hone'n' the other side. Once he'd hit

both sides, he flipped the stone to the smooth side and repeated the process.

"Don't you need to soak that stone first?"

"I already did when you were down at the river and while
we were talking."

"Why?"

"I figured the ax was probably too dull."

"Too dull?"

"Well we ain't using it to split wood now are we."

Jessup sat the ax and whetstone down and rolled up the
left sleeve of his shirt. He reached for the ax and carefully
shaved a small hair patch from his forearm.

"That should do it. Sharp as a Harvard graduate."

The thought of Eric and his pistol splashed, and I considered the likelihood that Jessup were 'bout to piece-hack me.
If only I had the knife, but, as far as I knowed, it remained
bloody on the floor 'side the lambed pig. 'fore my imagina-
tion ran 'way, Jessup posted and palmed me the fresh-sharp
ax. The motion 'peared odd religious or ritual like a priest
hand'n' out the host or something sacred. I took the handle
in both hands. I could defend now. I could even swing at
Jessup if it came to that. That settled me a bit and I realized
that for a while now my legs had steadied and I were tune'n'
no signs of rubber.

"Go on."

Jessup nodded toward the cabin door.

"Go on?"

"You have to do it, it's really the safest bet."

"Do what?"

"You got to chop that corpse up."

"What?"

Jessup seemed to be lose'n' patience, but facts were I
hadn't no notion what he were strat'n'.

"Remember, you have to walk through Hell to get to
Heaven. The easy way is to get on your scooter and leave this
mess, but we've got to clean up our messes in this life if we
want things to work out. How long do you think that dead

guy's going to be in this cabin before someone finds him and starts looking into who jacked him in the gut? How long before they realize that the runaway child of the deceased owner of this cabin is missing? Two plus two and you're not just a runaway, you're a fugitive and a murderer. Now go on and get to work."

"How's the ax gonna help?"

"You ever try to burn a big log in a fireplace? No. You split it, and it burns better."

I were start'n' upon the strat.

"I'm not gonna burn down my father's cabin?"

"You spilled the milk, not me."

"No, I mean I'm not ask'n' you to do it for me. I'm say'n' it ain't gonna happen at all. No one is gonna torch this cabin."

"What about the dead man?"

"What 'bout him?"

▲ ▼ ▲

It took some more convince'n', and I even hurled once, but eventually I fulfilled the RQD and transed the cabin-inside to a literal blood-mess.

Future tense, when I cracked the Shelley I low trembled at:

> *As I looked on him, his countenance expressed the utmost extent of malice and treachery. I thought with a sensation of madness on my promise of creating another like to him, and trembling with passion, tore to pieces the thing on which I was engaged.*

I were in the Beaver CC library. I book-dropped. My eyes room-darted. No one had noticed. Yet the memory of the deed were evoked and the fear of discovery 'turned. I weren't no Victor. No, I were the creature. I RQD Victor to build, not destroy. Yet I were Victor too. I retrieved the book, found my spot and cracked:

*Remember that I have power; you believe yourself
miserable, but I can make you so wretched that the
light of day will be hateful to you. You are my cre-
ator, but I am your master; obey!*

I glued it and foot-bounced to exhale tension. Shelly
knowed. She had to have knowed what it were like. I too sea-
tossed the dark night when I eyed the gut-mess and bone-
splinter and blood-paste and while I flamed evidence into
uncaptured smoke, Victor drowned his in the Irish sea.
'gardless, we both PTSDed—PTSDed like I ain't never 'mag-
ined. Nightmares and tremors assimilated normal and altho
my legs steadied reliable for longer episodes, my long hair
tangled and knotted and my girl tits sagged like a grandmother's. When I weren't dream'n' of the heat, the cage, and
the resurrection of the lambed pig, I were wood-wander'n'
aimless, bump'n' 'gainst trees and trip'n' over roots. I
grubbed virtually nothing for days and I would have wasted
'cept for bitter acorns, pine cones and worms that I force-
swallowed when I hit so close to collapse that I were will'n'
to gorge any potential. Jessup had ratcheted in the spark
plug post the fire, and Tessie had sealed the leaky canoe, but
when the cabin and all her contents flamed, I couldn't bring
myself to scooter-off or to canoe downstream. Jessup
skedaddled and sans a cabin and its contents, all I had were
the knife I fished off the floor and the duffle which at that
point merely served as a filthy-clothes repository.

It rained several times over those aimless days, and no
matter how much I stumbled, I spun circles back to the
damp cabin ash. The fire had burned hot and tall for 'most
an entire day. I fretted the smoke would 'tract 'tention and
bring 'dditional company, so I stashed a bit 'way from the
incinerate and lodged into a honeysuckle-tangle. From this
lookout, I plopped with my knife ready for any curious rubbernecks sniff'n' the smoke source. None popped and by
nightfall the fire set to embers and pop flames. The surround

trees and brush were green and damp 'nough to not catch
and the fire contained. Under darkness, I 'merged from my
hovel and perimeter paced the incinerate ruins. Everything
were still smolder and tiny flames popped up here and there
'fore extinguish'n' as quick as they 'peared. Sans the cabin,
the area 'peared large and open and flat and I were 'minded
of a campsite where a thru-hiker might tent-pop, unroll a
bag and pass a serenity night, yet, quick-swap the thought of
the facts wiped the serene and I shivered.

Aimless after the seventh circle on the seventh day, I
rolled in the cabin ash and hit paranoid 'bout the scooter
and the canoe. Perhaps that were why I couldn't crank nothing but circles. Clues on the scene. I mounted the scooter
and fired her with one swift kick. A smoke plume popped
and a bang backfire startled me, but I calmed and motored
the scooter to the river bank. I lifted off and ran it into the
Allegheny. The bike gurgled and air-bubbled as it submerged. Next I canoe-flipped. Tessie had left it unchained. I
loaded the supplies and oars into the belly and drug it to the
water where I 'llowed it to drift free. Facts is the scooter
might be findable near the bank but the canoe is either sank
or half to Mexico present tense. I reck it's sank, but I don't
know certain. With that out the way, my circle-back broke
straight and I continued aimless but cabin-distanced.

Some nights were cold and I shivered, and some days
were mud and damp. I trodded on. I had no strat 'cept to
separate the evidence from me, and that's what I were
'tempt'n' when the grave digger uncovered me crashed in the
cemetery with my duffle-pillow overlay'n' my father's marker. Facts is that I never 'tended to trek my father's marker,
and I's got no idea how I paced more than fifty miles distance from the cabin to lay crashed on my father's tomb, but
that's where I got near sliced with a gas trimmer 'fore the
grave digger stumbled over me. He thought I were a hobo
bum and soft PKed me with a steel toe 'fore order'n' me to
beat it, but when he eyed the girl tits and the tangle hair, he
figured something different were hit and he 'ssisted me to

the tool shed and served up black coffee. I wolfed four glazed and sucked a water jug 'sides the coffee. The grave digger tarp-wrapped me 'gainst the shiver and 'tempted to ID me. I silenced but pocket-dug the gold coin Tumult had gifted and offered it in exchange for hush. The grave digger pocketed the coin and rang the heat anyway. Fact, never trust no grave digger. They don't want to be no grave digger. They's most down-low ex-cons and poppers and I 'magine my gold coin went for a bag and a bottle and present tense it's deep street-buried and that's shame 'cause that were collaboration and now I's got nothing but my facts and that ain't move'n' my token to Boardwalk.

'least the grave digger didn't try no porno-perv. I were either too scraggly or he were not no perv or maybe both, but he didn't porno-perv me so that's plus one even tho he banked my coin and double crossed. I didn't know he'd rung the heat till one motored up to the shed. When I smelled that skunk, I 'tempted sprint but I were in no shape to 'scape no one and the grave digger easy tripped me. I faced a carved-angel-stone and woke to Father Antonio 'tempt'n' to fit a wafer 'tween my lips. My mother were there too and I quick-ly realized I were hospitalized.

"He has risen."

Father Antonio proclamated when my eyes popped.

"The boy has risen."

Father Antonio continued lip-jam'n' the wafer, and I sided to 'void. My mother fell on me and bawled 'bout rock'n' joy. Father Antonio gentled her off and after I consented to down the wafer, they both plopped.

"My son, you gave your mother and I quite a scare. You know it's lucky that the man who found you notified the authorities. There's no telling what someone else might have done with a youngster in your condition. Yes, you're lucky your guardian angel was watching over you."

I silenced and eyed the room. It were an ordinary hospital semi-private but the other bed were vacant. Father Antonio noticed me eye'n' the empty.

"God called his lamb to heaven last night so you have the room to yourself for now."

"Happy Easter, Paul Joseph. You're the best Easter basket I've ever gotten."

"Easter?"

"Yes, son, it's Easter Sunday. Well at least for another hour or so."

As I focused, I slight 'membered face'n' the angle-stone. I fingered my bandage head and realized my long hair were gone. I quickly fingered to my front and hit regular dude pecs. The girl tits were gone. I wanted to finger down low but my mother and Father Antonio were eye'n'.

"Whatever you were taking son seems to have worn off. The doctors say that other than your head wound and some dehydration and malnourishment, that you're back to normal."

"Back to normal?"

"Yes, back to normal."

"Anthony and I have been very worried. We had no idea where you ran too. And in the condition you were in... Like Anthony said, you're one lucky young man. There's no telling what could have happened to you. But now that you're back I'm very happy. I was so worried that I wouldn't get to say a proper goodbye."

"A proper goodbye?"

A nurse popped and vitaled me. She claimed that I RQD rest and that a doc would be hit'n' in the AM. My mother and Father Antonio left palm'n' hands and the nurse hit back and sunk a syringe in the drip that crashed me quick.

When I came back, two docs and an authority wack hovered over. One doc were a medical and the other were a therapeutic. The authority wack were a detective and he spilled first.

"Son, we found a knife in your duffle that has traces of human blood on it. We ran some tests and we know the blood is not yours. We're going to need to ask you a few questions."

"With all due respect detective, the boy's suffered a head injury and has been through a lot, could we hold the questions for a bit? Son, I'm Doctor Jim and I'm a therapist. I work here at St. Luke's. How are you?"

The medical doc stethoscoped me and fingered the head bandage.

"Look gentlemen, as long as the boy is in this hospital bed, he's under my care. Whatever business you two have with him will have to wait until I say he's medically stable. With a head injury like his, we need some time to assess and monitor. Anything he says right now might be a byproduct of the injury and certainly could not be considered reliable."

"Doctor, this here's an open crime scene in my book and I must insist that I be permitted to speak with the boy."

"Now come on, I'm the only one here with therapeutic training. This boy's been through tremendous grief. Do you two even know that his father died not too long ago. Give the kid a break. Let me speak with him for a while and then detective, if you insist on raking him through the coals, he'll at least be more stable."

A no-nonsense nurse hit and shuffled out all three of the lumps.

"Now son, as long as I'm on duty, you're going to have some peace and quiet. You need rest. Geez, the nerve of men, they never give anyone a chance to breathe."

She vitaled me, pillow-flipped and held a straw to my lips. I sucked some chill-water, eye-shut and crashed. I came back after dark and 'gain my mother and Father Antonio were plopped bedside. My mother were aglow and Father Antonio were giggle-whisper'n'.

"Paul Joseph, your mother and I have something to tell you. We know this isn't the best timing, but we want you to hear it from us first and since other people already know it, we decided to tell you now."

My mother leaned in and forehead-pecked while Father Antonio spilled.

"My son, your mother is a remarkable woman and over the years we have grown close. In fact, we are more than close. One might say, in the words of the youth today, that we are a couple. And obviously this has created several ethical and moral compromises, but we have prayed over it and our hearts, guided by the Lord our Savior, tell us that it would be sinful to deny our true feelings. I've asked the Bishop for a leave of absence and he has consented. Your mother and I are leaving tomorrow for Italy. Your little running away stunt prevented us from looping you in on the planning. I'm sorry about that, but really you did this to yourself."

My mother leaned in.

"Paul Joseph, you know I love you, but I also know that you want me to be happy. I was uncertain about my feelings and what to do about them, but with lots of prayer and then with your drugs, deception, and defiance, what could I do? I can't stay here and attempt to mother a juvenile delinquent. I'm sure to you this seems sudden, but Anthony and I have been in love for a long time and then you ran away and we had no idea if we'd ever see you again. Now you just turn back up. Surely you can't expect everything to just be the same as it was when you left. I'm sorry, but the world goes on. I am glad that you showed up before we left though. I was feeling guilty about leaving without seeing you one last time."

I eyed both. I were fatigue and clouds and not certain what I 'eared correct. Father Antonio shoulder-palmed to strike me 'lert.

"Son, I know this might be hitting you like a shock, but really it's all for the best. Imagine your mother and I in a relationship here in town. You'd be the center of attention and scandal. No, it's best for us to go away. At least for the time being. After all, you're seventeen now and going to be a senior next year. You're old enough to care for yourself. I think your little drug experiment proves that."

Seventeen? I were seventeen. My birthday had hit while I were on the skedaddle. With the mess, I slipped it.

"Now don't think we haven't made certain arrangements. When you get better here, we are discharging you to a drug treatment center."

My mother piped.

"It's the best one in all of Pittsburgh. It's run by the Communita Cenaclo and they even offer Calix. You'll be in good hands there as you work through the program. In fact, I think you've already met their liaison, Doctor Jim. He's making all the arrangements and will see that you get safely settled in at Our Lady of Hope."

"Now son, I know the future is cloudy for you, but with God's help, you can work through the program and come out a new man, ready for a fresh start."

"Paul Joseph, the program requires a twelve month residential commitment so you'll be eighteen when you finish. They have their own school, and you'll be able to graduate on time and then, when you're discharged, we'll see where we all are and figure it out."

It were all overload. Drug rehab, the detective, my mother and Father Antonio flip'n' to Italy, my return to dude. I suddenly missed Tumult and Tessie and Jessup. Facts is they were the lumps who aided best even if I didn't realize it at the time. My mother tight-hugged me and spewed love, and Father Antonio palmed my hand. The two of them skedaddled palm'n' and I ain't eyed neither since. I got two postcards. One from the Vatican and one from Sicily. I ain't got the faintest of their current locale and fact is that I no longer care.

I s'pose I need to dig here 'cause that's what a therapeutic is and a mother ditch'n' to Italy with a priest ain't regular, so here's the hole I shoveled. I love my mother 'cause lumps love their mothers. It's facts. But we can love and bust simultaneously which Therapeutic Kate learnt me and that's the ground I'm post'n'. When my father cancered, my mother tipped her hand. Her three tops spun out God, my father, and Father Antonio. As an adolescent, I made the faulty assumption that I were the top of my mother's list, but present tense I eye I were no higher than fourth. You might post I sweated this too, but I'd eyed lots by then and were combat-hard. 'sides, my mother weren't no ally. She were convinced of drugs and Calix and them were both false facts. So facts is we all love our mothers but we don't all RQ them 'round especially if they's loon 'nough to hitch Father Antonio. I ain't left field here as much as I'm shallow field. 'gardless, let's get back to the rail.

▲ ▼ ▲

'bout three months after I flipped eighteen, I got a snail-legal spill'n' that I present tense were a homeowner and that there were a trust to cover incidentals. 'parently Father Antonio stuffed his mattress and my father pulled a life policy like he knowed he'd early kick. 'tween the two, I were cash and shelter for present tense. I termed the rehab with no gain but I knowed how to pretend religious and at least got clean sheets and three squares. The rehab spun positive in that I did RQ a safe house to adjust back to dude and side-line-eye what were break'n'. What Father Antonio and my mother dropped silent were what were 'ready pop'n' 'bout the sitch. Seems they got eyed in'propriate in the sanctuary and it scandled big even to the local six o'clock. My first year at Sacred Heart, Father Paul cracked as a pedo-perv and the heat perp-walked him cuffed down the Sacred Heart halls. That rocked foundations and school enrollment dropped 'nough to reclass the team D2 which were a bless 'cause we could never blast St. Albert's who hoisted the D1 state four straight. Facts is Father Paul's pedo-perv hurt some but aided on the pitch. Social blew with pics of the hallway perp-walk and that's how the local six o'clock picked it and spun it outside the walls. Ever since, the local six o'clock were eye'n' for 'dditional Sacred Heart dirty laundry. When the alter boy posted pics of Father Antonio's sanctuary-fondle, it were only small potatoes till the local six dug up my girl tits and long hair and runaway and then it sensationalized and that viraled. Social 'course flipped me as MIA and in less than 24 every lump from PA to the Lone Star knowed 'bout the girl tits and long hair. I ain't certain what they knowed 'bout the shrunken area, but the influencers hyped their speculation. There weren't no pics but lumps pulled soccer clips and deep faked a girl. Even Jessica shamed when she socialed it and eventually ghosted but first she watered social spec with spills 'bout our last days. I didn't know none of this that PM when Father Antonio and my mother Italy-eloped, but Therapeutic Jim spilled me up to present tense in the AM and that noon the discharge affected and Therapeutic Jim escorted me to the rehab transport.

▲ ▼ ▲

'nother sidebar facts: since you're crack'n' this therapeutic that ain't meant for public consumption, you should know it ain't inked at seventeen in the rehab. I inked it 'cause Therapeutic Kate thought it'd hit me good, and perhaps it has, but if you ain't Therapeutic Kate and you's cracking this, then I knows now that they ain't trustworthy 'cause if they ain't the leak who is? Beaver CC hitched me to Therapeutic Kate 'cause they classified me as potentially self-harmful and RQD an eval to sustain enrollment. Facts is I weren't no cutter and present tense ain't no suicide neither. I'm too Heinz 57 for that. Just 'cause I popped at the Beaver CC skunk show and spilled from the roof, I weren't gonna jump. Those facts is flipped. I were eye'n' the SJWs. They was all libs and 'cuse'n' me of phobia, but you's 'ready know from my contra that that ain't the road I walk. The Beaver CC pseudo-heat broke the skunk and I climbed down and that's when the Beaver CC RQD an eval. The eval turned no danger to self but Therapeutic Kate spilled that Beaver CC would fund us and I kept hit'n' them and them's who dreamed up this write'n' process even tho I ain't no writer which is obvious facts by this therapeutic, but I inked it all and scribed in the leaked parts 'fore it were leaked just in-case Therapeutic Kate or some other lump spilled it and if you's just Therapeutic Kate then you can ignore these leak speculations, but if you's some unauthorized lump, I write this for you to know that I know that you're crack'n' this but you ain't got no right.

Facts is that I cogitate that this therapeutic that you ain't even s'pose to be crack'n' is 'nough contra to satisfy that I ain't no loon and that I's got no comment on girls be'n' boys and boys be'n' girls. It just happened to me for a short and then stopped. I ain't a mouthpiece of nothing and that's facts. 'gardless Therapeutic Kate recommends that even if I ain't no loon nor spokesperson pro nor con, I might sabbatical from Beaver CC and bunk a bit at the nuthouse 'cause I'd be safer there than out where the heat is still detective'n' the human blood on the knife. Therapeutic Kate advised I ghost social and 'llow fizzle which it sorta is but there's still past tense and it don't erase so the weasel pops a head here and there like the skunk at Beaver CC but mostly that's cooked. The heat ain't so easy tho. They ain't pressed nothing 'cause they can't hit a crime sans a lambed pig and altho I spilled 'bout the lambed pig, they couldn't lock it without no victim so present tense I'm a person of interest and the needle is stuck there 'less discovery. The heat 'tempted me cut'n' trail to the crime scene, but I couldn't pin it exactly and eventually they uncled and let me 'lone, but present tense when they trip on a lambed John Doe, they motor to the nuthouse and raise eye brows.

▲▼▲

I utilized some trust to fund Beaver CC but I was gonna drop anyway 'cause SJWs keep skunk'n' me and 'sides the courses slept. 'cept for crack'n' Kafka and Shelley, it were totally impractical. Facts is I probably would not have never played Beaver CC 'cept for Bruno who I hitch at rehab. He weren't no addict neither. He joyed opioids and RQD a come off so the lumps keyed him in and we roomed. Past tense he danced the pitch and in rehab we'd work back-heel volleys in the rec yard. He were ten or so older and a popper but he steadied solid skill. Bruno rocked sketch'n' and paint'n' and his creations were good. He learnt me that the key were shapes. He didn't know nothing 'bout my dad's cheap repo, but he eyed me *Christina's World* in an art book he owned and pointed that it were all triangles. Seems he didn't even eye no cripple girl or barn nor nothing, just triangles and color. Bruno spilled that girls and barns and flowers ain't there. It's just shapes and colors. Authentic artists eye it that way at least. Regular lumps eye girls and barns and flowers and even tho I scribed this entire therapeutic san no dream analytic, that PM after I got learnt by Bruno, I dreamed a dream 'bout triangles. I only mention it 'cause it were one of those dreams you 'ear 'bout where a math-lump solution-dreams a complex mathematical or a music-lump melody-dreams a gold record. It were an insight dream and in the dream I eyed everything' like Bruno learnt me as triangles. Paintings and landscapes and lumps all were there, but I could triangle overlay them and comprehend every triangle lock'n' 'gether. Even that *Christina's World* print from 'bove my mantle sudden were all triangles and the symmetry rocked Eden.

I ain't never dreamed of no triangles since that night, and I don't know how it could've been connected with nothing. Jessup spewed 'bout Hell and Heaven 'fore the flame'n' and the aimlessness, and I ain't eye'n' any connection with that and triangles. But, since this is a therapeutic I figured I'd include that fact here at the end in case it rocks important.

▲ ▼ ▲